MAPALOGUE

Monster High

Normie High

Also by Shannon Hale

EVER AFTER HIGH

The Storybook of Legends

The Unfairest of Them All

A Wonderlandiful World

Once Upon a Time:
A Story Collection

The Legend of Shadow High

SHANNON HALE
& DEAN HALE

Little, Brown and Company

New York Boston

Map illustrations by Virginia Allyn.
Cover design by Christina Quintero. Cover illustration by Erwin Madrid.
Interior design by Véronique Lefèvre Sweet.

Little, Brown and Company
Hachette Book Group
1290 Avenue of the Americas, New York, NY 10104
Visit us at LBYR.com
everafterhigh.com
monsterhigh.com

First Edition: October 2017

Little, Brown and Company is a division of Hachette Book Group, Inc.
The Little, Brown name and logo are trademarks of Hachette Book Group, Inc.

The publisher is not responsible for websites (or their content) that are not owned by the publisher.

Library of Congress Cataloging-in-Publication Data
Names: Hale, Shannon, author. | Hale, Dean 1972- author.
Title: The legend of Shadow High / Shannon Hale and Dean Hale.
Description: First edition. | New York : Little, Brown, 2017. | Series: Monster High/Ever After High
Identifiers: LCCN 2017009561| ISBN 9780316352826 (hardback) | ISBN 9780316352840 (ebook) | ISBN 9780316352833 (library edition ebook)
Subjects: | BISAC: JUVENILE FICTION / Media Tie-In. | JUVENILE FICTION / Social Issues / Friendship. | JUVENILE FICTION / Toys, Dolls, Puppets.
Classification: LCC PZ7.H13824 Le 2017 | DDC [Fic]--dc23
LC record available at https://lccn.loc.gov/2017009561

ISBNs: 978-0-316-35282-6 (paper over board), 978-0-316-35284-0 (ebook)

Printed in the United States of America

WOR

10 9 8 7 6 5 4 3 2 1

For our royal monsters Gabe & Levi

CHAPTER 1

IT'S MORNING AT MONSTER HIGH. THE OLD building sits up on Monster Hill like…like… uh, I'm trying to think of a good simile here. I studied similes last semester, but I'm still new at narrating. It sat on the hill like a big, dark birthday cake? Like a hairless rock giant? Like a fancy pointed hat worn by particularly well-behaved geographical features?

Ugh, I'm already messing this up! I'm not supposed to say *I*, for starters. *I* am the Narrator, not a character in this story. Let me start over.[1]

---

[1] *Psst.* Hey, Reader. Yeah, you. Hi, I'm Brooke Page, the Narrator for this story! Since it's against Narrator Rules for me to talk directly to you, when I need to tell you something, I'll just whisper it down here in the footnotes, okay?

Ahem. It's morning at Monster High. The spiders are humming, the termites are chittering, the wind is sliding through the shutters with an eerie whistle. A beautiful day.

Oh, and hey! There are Draculaura and Frankie Stein! Walking through the massive front doors, carrying their bags on their shoulders, with absolutely no idea of the epic, possibly world-ending story that's about to unravel.

Draculaura is a vampire—obviously. Pale pink skin, long fangs, glossy black hair with pink highlights, a pink-and-black dress with polka dots. Frankie has mint-green skin and black hair shocked with thick white stripes. You can see the seams in her arms and legs where her father, Frankenstein, stitched her together.

Both girls are super excited. You can tell by the way they're walking—a hop in their step, nearly skipping. But Frankie is also nervous. You can tell from that shiver in her hands and tremor in her chin.[2]

"Don't forget the intro music," says Draculaura.

"I've got it queued up on my iCoffin," Frankie

2 Plus, I can guess their thoughts. Well, at the moment, just Frankie's, so that's why she's the point-of-view character in this chapter. It's a Narrator thing.

says, holding up her coffin-shaped phone as they pass the coffin-shaped lockers.[3] "Have you got the—"

"Sound effects?" says Draculaura, pulling a portable keyboard from her pack. "Check!"

"And the—"

"Images?" says Draculaura. "The photo slide show is totes on my iCoffin."

"Right. But don't forget the special effects," says Frankie, handing Draculaura the Portable EffecTacular that Frankie made in her lab. The size of a toaster, it creates all sorts of monstrous effects.

"Are you sure we should use the EffecTacular?" asks Draculaura. "The other students won't have smoke clouds and ice storms in their presentations. I didn't have much time to practice with it and"—Draculaura plays with the hem of her skirt—"it seems kinda…umm…scary…but not in a good way?"

"Well, maybe we don't *need* them," says Frankie, "but they'll make our presentation voltageous."

---

3 Coffins: It's a monster thing.

"Well, of course! But getting back to the dangerous part…Um, maybe our presentation will still be great even without the EffecTacular?"

"Great?" Frankie's neck bolts buzz with excitement. "But great isn't enough. Not near enough. We're the cofounders of Monster High. They're going to expect something…something *amazing*!"

"Oh, okay, I'm sure you're right."

Today their history class will give their oral presentations on the creation of Monster High. And since Frankie and Draculaura kinda, sorta actually founded the school, Frankie feels a wee bit of pressure to kinda, sorta actually be *spooktacular*.[4]

They slide into their seats just as Mr. Rotter starts the class.

"Let's see," he says, rubbing his fingers over his pallid gray forehead, "I believe Marshall is up first."

The small swamp monster slurps his way to the front of the class, blinks his one eye, and shrugs

---

4 I, for one, am still geeking out about getting to narrate a story about *the* Frankie Stein and *the* Draculaura! I'm a huge fan, but don't tell them. I'm trying to play it cool.

the tangled knot of his thorny vine hair out of the way.

"So…" says Marshall. "I, uh, lived in a swamp. I ate swamp stuff, you know? Did swamp things. Then Frankie and Drac found me and said, 'Hey, we started a school called Monster High and, hey, you should come and learn stuff and not be alone all the time.' So I did."

Marshall sits back down.

"Thank you, Marshall," says Mr. Rotter, lids blinking slowly over his black eyes. "Next time work on details and listing references, okay? Well, I hope Draculaura and Frankie will be an example to you all of a proper oral presentation."

"You bet we will!" Draculaura says.

She smiles at Frankie, her fangs glinting.

Frankie smiles back.

No pressure, no pressure, Frankie tells herself. *Just be amazing. How hard can it be to be amazing?*

Frankie joins Draculaura in front of the class and gulps. So many eyes look back! Some blue, some green, some black, some bulging, some wiggling on the ends of tentacles. All staring. At her.

Moving to Monster High and making so many friends has been Frankie's fondest scream come true. But sometimes she still feels like the lonely ghoul hidden inside her father's laboratory.

From the back row, her ghoulfriend Clawdeen Wolf gives her a claws-up and a toothy smile.[5]

Frankie returns the thumbs-up, relieved that her hand doesn't take it as an invitation to wander off in that direction...without the rest of her. She clears her throat. No time for nerves—Draculaura is depending on her!

"So. Um. Once upon a time..." Frankie starts.

The class giggles. *Once upon a time* is how fairytales start, and monsters definitely don't believe in fairytales.

Their laughs give Frankie more confidence, a sign that she's being entertaining, at least. "Once upon a time," she says, pressing PLAY on her iCoffin. Mysterious music fills the room. "There was a vampire named Draculaura...."

Draculaura presses the first button on the EffecTacular—FRANKIE'S MIST POTION. A cloud of

5 Clawdeen: daughter of werewolves. Seriously cool ghoul.

smoke billows out of the little machine. Through it walks Draculaura, dramatic, her hands up.

"Ta-da!" she says.

The students clap. A few, the ones who don't enjoy breathing a little swamp gas, cough on the smoke.

"Uh, sorry," says Frankie, fanning it away.

She begins to tell the tale of how Draculaura lived with her father, Dracula, in a big, ancient house on a hill for many, many years till the night she went out flying in bat form and first met Frankie. They both had been longing for a life like the Normie teenagers had: attending high school, fanging out with friends, just living in the open. So they started to search for other monsters like them who'd been hiding from the Normies.[6] Monsters who were aching for a different kind of life.

"First we went to the swamps," says Frankie. "There had to be monsters there, right?"

"Right!" says Marshall from his seat.

---

6 In case you don't know, Normies are what the monsters call normal people (i.e., not monsters). Monster history has shown that whenever Normies know monsters are real and might, for instance, be living on a hilltop close to their town, they flip out, and things tend to go very badly for the monsters. So, long ago, the monster community decided that hiding from the Normies was the best solution.

"And so, one Tuesday night..." says Frankie.

Draculaura plays a creepy sound effect on her keyboard and presses the WET FROG SMELL button on the EffecTacular. A panel slides open, revealing a small, wet frog. An equally small fan begins to whir behind the frog, blowing its humid smell out to the class. But right then, Frankie's iCoffin battery runs out and the music stops. She touches her finger to it to jolt it with electricity. Oops. A bright spark leaps from the iCoffin, through the moist air, and into the EffecTacular. Turns out homemade special effects machines do not handle surprise electricity very well. All the little hatches of the device open at once, and its living contents—including the tiny frog, a swarm of pyramid moths, and one very excited scorpion—make an escape.

The class screams. The scorpion trots across Mr. Rotter's desk and begins to happily sting the stacks of paper.

"Loose beasts!" yells Frankie. "Drac, get the scorpion bag!"

"I got it," says Draculaura, pulling out a canvas bag labeled SCORPIONS. Oh no, Frankie must have brought the wrong bag. Instead of being a nice, empty place to put an escaped scorpion, it is full of *extra* scorpions, which scuttle out and scamper toward the students. More screams. Students run, crawl, and slither through the door.[7]

"Sorry!" yells Frankie as she chases the leaping frog. "We have to slow them down! Try the…uh…. the SIMULATED ICY NORTH button on the EffecTacular!"

"Is it still working?"

"Here, let me," says Frankie, taking the EffecTacular from Draculaura. She aims it at the scorpion on the desk and presses the button just as Mr. Rotter runs toward it with the classroom pyre extinguisher. The Icy North spray hits the extinguisher, which pops like a balloon filled with liquid ice.

"No!" the girls scream.

Mr. Rotter is frozen in a block of ice from the neck down. He tries to take a step, but he tips and falls face-first with a *thud*.

"Ow," he says, his mouth pressed against the floor. A scorpion scampers over him and out the door.

---

7 Like, literally *through* the door. Usually, monsters remember to open doors first. Usually.

"Sorry," says Frankie. "Sorry? Um, really, really sorry."

The classroom is empty, a swamp monster–shaped hole in the door. Just Clawdeen remains, capturing the last scorpion and stuffing it into her backpack for safekeeping.

Mr. Rotter mumbles something incoherent from the floor.

Frankie clears her throat. "Um, Mr. Rotter? Is this a good time to show you our big finale?"

Later, Frankie and Draculaura are in their room, slumped on their beds.[8] Their clothes smell like smoke. Their shoes are wet from melted ice.

"We have only two days," Frankie mutters.

"Yep," Draculaura mutters.

"It took us a *week* to get ready for this report," Frankie mutters.

"Yep," Draculaura mutters, continuing the whole muttering trend.

---

8 If you wonder why we skipped ahead, it's because I had to grab a snack. Now you know: When you're reading a book and time jumps forward, the reason is probably that the Narrator had to take a break or, like, go to bed or something.

They are too despondent to do anything besides slump on their beds and mutter. Mr. Rotter has given them forty-eight hours to come up with a new oral report on a high school—but it can't be on Monster High, because, he said, "apparently your Monster High reports include frostbite and scorpion assault."

"I'm so sorry, Drac," says Frankie. "I don't know why I packed extra scorpions. I was just worried something would go wrong, and…and I should've let you do the ice one—"

Draculaura giggles a little. "Now that it's over? Mr. Rotter as a giant ice pop was top ten–level funny."

Frankie laughs. Then sighs. "I just wanted it to be really amazing. I guess we'll have to do our report on—"

"Normie High," Draculaura finishes. "It's the only other high school I know anything about. But we can't go down to the village to research it in person. My dad would flip his coffin if we went any-where near the Normies."

"Besides, everyone already knows about Normies," says Frankie. "We need to do something different to make up for that…that *monstrous* disaster."

Draculaura perks up. "Come on," she says, taking Frankie's hand. She gets to the door of the room before she realizes Frankie isn't attached to her hand.[9]

"Wait for the rest of me!" says Frankie, jogging after her. She sews her hand back to her wrist while they run into the principal's[10] office, which contains his massive personal library.

"Dad always says, 'Anything you need you can find in a book,'" says Draculaura.

"What if I need a cheese sandwich?" Frankie whispers. Her stomach rumbles with hunger. In all her excitement for their presentation, Frankie forgot to eat breakfast. Draculaura grabs an apple off the desk and tosses it across the room. Frankie catches it and takes a bite while examining the shelves.

Soon she's absorbed in reading gold-lettered spines and searching tables of contents for anything about high school.

"Hey," says Frankie. "This book says that ages ago, before monsters went into hiding, there was another school for monsters, so this isn't the first Monster High!"

9 Don't be alarmed, Reader. Limbs coming loose is a thing that happens to Frankie.
10 Dracula is the principal of the school. How fangtastic is that?

It would make a fangtastic report…if only Mr. Rotter hadn't forbidden them from presenting on Monster High again.

"Look at this!" says Drac.

What she's holding can hardly be called a book. It's just a bundle of papers sewn together with waxed thread, the parchment so old it's turned brown. Written in smudged watery ink on the front are the words *Shadow High*.[11]

Frankie reads the title out loud and then rubs her arms. "I didn't know I was physically capable of getting goosebumps, but I just did."

"Me too," says Draculaura. "There's something about that name…*Shadow High*…."

Frankie flips through the pages, but they're blank.

"Why would your dad have a blank book? Is it a diary no one ever used?"

"It's totes old," says Drac. "Maybe the ink faded."

"I dunno," says Frankie, peering at the pages.

---

11 Oh no. Here we go. I can feel it. This is where the real plot starts. The reason no other Narrators will touch this story. I'd warn the girls, but even if interfering with the characters weren't hugely against Narrator Rules, they can't hear me. Only you, Reader, know what I narrate. Oh, and also a couple of very unique characters, whom I have a feeling we'll meet soon.

"Looks to me like someone erased it. On purpose. And there I go, getting goosebumps again."

They run to find Dracula, who is having a cup of tea with Clawdeen's mom on the veranda, overlooking the cemetery.

"Shadow High? I've never heard of it." Dracula rubs his arms. "*Ooh*, did the temperature just drop? I'm suddenly chilly. And I thought I was already the *coolest* dad ever."[12]

He laughs heartily. Clawdeen's mom joins in.

"I mean…there is a *bite* in the air," he says, smiling with his fangs showing. The two adults laugh again.

Draculaura rolls her eyes. "Yeah…funny, Dad. But anyhoo, about Shadow High?"

"Hmm…Shadow High…You say you found it in *my* library? You know, I think I used to know—"

Dracula is interrupted by a distant plopping noise.

"What was that sound?" he says.

"Oh dear," says Clawdeen's mom. "I hope the pipes aren't leaking."

They both get up and go to check.

---

12 Dad jokes, amirite? They seem to be universal, no matter whether the dad is vampire or Normie or Narrator.

The girls look at each other. Draculaura sighs. "Dad jokes, amirite?" she says.[13]

The girls rush back down, nearly tackling Mr. Mum-Ho-Tep, who is sweeping the floor at the base of the stairs. Mr. Mum-Ho-Tep is so old he's worn down to almost nothing. His hair under his janitor cap billows around him, thinner than cobwebs, and his skin is like paper. When he exhales, he nearly disappears when viewed from the side. Frankie reasons that anyone who's lived that long must have heard of everything, even—

"Shadow High?" he whispers in response to her question. "That name sounds familiar. Let me think...."

He taps his temple in concentration, but just then a *plop* noise sounds from...somewhere.

"What was that plop?" he asks in his raspy voice. "It broke my concentration."

"I don't know," says Draculaura. She smiles sweetly. "Now, you were saying—"

"About Shadow High?" Frankie prompts.

"Ah, yes. Shadow High. That name is ominous,

---

13 Omigosh, that's exactly what I said a minute ago! I bet me and Drac would be friends if she knew I existed!

isn't it? I'd bet my very last toenail I've heard it before.... It's on the edge of my memory, or in a memory that has somehow been erased from my mind. But if I concentrate..." He closes his eyes.

Plop. Plop.

"Upside-down pyramids!" he exclaims. "What in the ancient world is that plopping sound? I have to find it!"

And off he goes, on the hunt for the plop.[14]

Frankie rubs her arms. They're speckled with— you guessed it—goosebumps.

"Does it almost seem like—" Draculaura starts.

"There's a random plopping noise whenever—" Frankie continues.

"We ask someone about..." Draculaura pauses, then whispers, "*Shadow High?*"

Frankie nods. "It's so mysterious! We have to get to the bottom of this."

"Are you sure we should?" says Draculaura. "Doesn't something about it seem...creepy?"

Frankie hesitates. First the goosebumps, and now she feels as if there are skeleton moths in her stomach.

---

14 Wait a sentence! What are all these plops? I'm as confused as you are, Reader.

She pulls her shirt up an inch, and through a seam in her waist a moth crawls out and flits away.

"But don't you think that this *Shadow High*"—she whispers the name—"might be the perfect subject for our report? Like it was just waiting for us to discover it!"

"You're right!" says Draculaura, straightening. "We're monsters. Things are supposed to be scared of *us*, not the other way around!"

Frankie nods. She can tell Draculaura is a little scared but pushing through it. Frankie is proud she's the BGF[15] of such a courageous monster. She stands up straighter while hopeful zaps of electricity travel up her spine.

"Shadow High does sound creepy-cool, doesn't it?" Frankie says. "Maybe it's some other, secret Monster High!"

Plop. Plop.

"Did you hear that plop?" asks Draculaura.

"Never mind the plop. I've got an idea."

15 BGF: Best Ghoulfriend Forever.

CHAPTER 2

MOM. DAD. I KNOW IT WAS YOU INTERRUPTING my narration with that plopping sound. Are you following me around? Where are you? Aha! Mom, I can see you hiding behind those vines and dangling participles.

Brooke, sweetie...

You too, Dad. Come out from behind the spoiler tree. Honestly, you're a terrible hider. I can totally see your shoes.

Brooke, honey ...

Hey, what's that thing you're holding? A vacuum or something?

No. It's … well, it's a Plop Device.

You mean a *plot* device? I learned about that. It's anything that helps move the story forward. Like, the temperature of the Three Bears' porridge is a plot device because it causes the bears to leave to let it cool, and then their absence makes it possible for Goldilocks to break in—

Yes, yes, you're very smart, Brooke, but this is … ahem, it's not a plot device. It's a Plop Device.

I've never heard of it.

Yeah … it's top secret. The characters in a story can't hear us speaking,[16] but they can hear the sounds this machine makes. Narrators aren't supposed to interfere in any way, of course—

But a plopping noise is such a small interference.

Yes, exactly. Sometimes a well-timed plopping noise can distract a character who is about to do something that might ruin the story.

Are you trying to distract the characters? Or stop the story from happening altogether? But why? What

16 Except for a couple of them, whom you'll meet soon!

is it that you don't want Frankie and Draculaura to discover? What is Shadow High?

Shhh! Don't even say those words. And please stop narrating! I don't want you anywhere near this story. It's too dangerous.

I don't get why you and the other Narrators don't want this story to be told. Draculaura and Frankie will do whatever they're going to do whether we narrate it or not.

But, Brooke—

Maybe I'm just a kid, but I know that every story deserves to be told. And if no one narrates this one, then the Readers will never know what happens! So if you won't do it, I will.

CHAPTER 3

Frankie Stein lived all her early life in a laboratory: covered windows; nice, clean concrete floors; flickering lights; and the comforting buzz of electricity. Endless books to read, gadgets to fiddle with, and contraptions to invent—like that electric flyswatter she wired up, or the automatic spoon...which more often than not missed her mouth and spooned cereal into her ear.

So it was mostly good! But also, it was *so* lonely.

Unlike all Normie kids and most monsters, Frankie wasn't born a baby who grew up into a teenager. She was *created* as a teenager. She woke up one day on a slab and had to figure out what *teenager* even meant. Frankie used to scour the Monster Web for information about Normie teenagers, peer through the slats of a lab window, and wish for friends who could understand how just creepy-cool life was.

And now at last she has those longed-for friends, especially her BGF, Draculaura. Far worse than having to go back into hiding again would be disappointing her friends. She's certain she let down Drac with the presentation. So what's a ghoul to do? Fix it!

In their bedroom, Frankie grabs the Mapalogue[17] from the closet and places the box on her desk.

"The Mapalogue? To find Shadow High?" says Draculaura. "That only works to locate monsters."

"Yeah, but what if Shadow High *is* monsters?" says Frankie. "It kinda sounds like it."

She opens the box, and the wooden map unfolds. It's smooth, polished by the fingers, claws, and tentacles of all the monsters who have used it over the centuries to find one another in a world full of Normies.

---

17 The Monster Mapalogue is like a monster detector, complete with a world map and a Skullette magical teleporting thingamabob.

Burned into the wood's surface are the borders and names of all the known places of the world.

The Mapalogue was how Frankie and Drac had found monsters hiding in various locations and then transported themselves there to deliver an invitation to Monster High. When they touched the Skullette token Draculaura now wore around her neck and spoke the words *Exsto monstrum* plus the monster's name, the Mapalogue could send them directly to that monster. It was how they found Cleo de Nile, daughter of the Mummy, hidden in her royal tomb home beneath the desert sands. And how they found Lagoona Blue, daughter of the sea monster, emerging from the surf to meet them beachside.

"The problem is we don't know anyone's name at Shadow High," says Draculaura.

"It's a school, right?" says Frankie. "There's got to be a principal."

Frankie shivers with excitement. Or maybe a jolt of all that loose electricity just surged through her body and bolted up her spine. Either way, it is clawesome having friends. Friends mean adventures in a world so much bigger than a boarded-up laboratory.

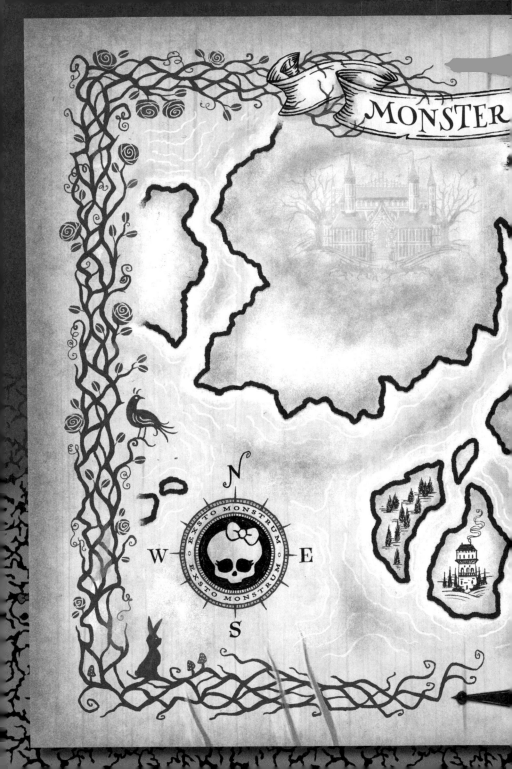

MONSTER

Frankie takes her friend's hand. Draculaura touches the Skullette pendant around her neck. They take a breath. And then—

Plop. Plop.

"What the…?"

"Seriously, what is that plopping sound?" says Draculaura.

"Let's just ignore it."

They hold hands again, touch the Skullette, look at the map, and together say, *"Exsto monstrum principal of Shadow High—"*

And they fall. But not out of Monster High and into Shadow High. Just onto their butts. On their bedroom floor. Not transported. They were knocked down by nothing.

"What just—"

"Did that—"

Their door swings open. Clawdeen pushes her voluminous brown hair out of her eyes.

"Ghouls, did you feel that?" says Clawdeen. "I think we just had an earthquake! I'm gonna go check on my little brothers."

And she bounds off just as quickly as she entered.

"That was—" Frankie starts.

"Creepy," Draculaura finishes.

They stand up, brush themselves off, and shrug. They aren't hurt. So they try it again. Hands held. Skullette touched. Deep breaths. As they speak, the plopping sounds return.[18]

"Exsto monstrum"—*plop, plop*—*"principal"*—*PLOP*—*"of Shadow"*—*plopplopplopplopplop*—*"High!"*

Almost before the words come out of their mouths, another tremor rolls beneath their feet. The stones of Monster High groan, the wood floor begins to buckle, the books on the shelves burst off like popping corn. And most ominously, the mirror on the wall cracks in two. Now Frankie is shivering for real. Two earthquakes in a row? That can't be a coincidence—

"Whoa!" exclaims Draculaura.

"What?" says Frankie.

"Look!"

"Look at what?"

"Whoa! Look! Whoa!"

Draculaura finally points at the map. Frankie gasps.

18 Honestly. My parents can be so weird sometimes.

MONSTER

Ever After High

EXSTO MONSTRUM
EXSTO MONSTRUM

N

W   E

S

"How…how did…but how did…" Frankie mumbles.

"I have no idea," Draculaura whispers.

The map, which was burned into the wood who knew how many centuries or even millennia ago, has changed. It's as if it has zoomed out and revealed that the places they know are only one small part of all the world. The map of their world is squished down in the corner. And new lands with new borders are burning into the wood right before their eyes. One particularly large continent-like part bears a name: EVER AFTER HIGH.

CHAPTER 4

EVER AFTER. THE LAND OF FAIRYTALES AND nursery rhymes, magical creatures and storybook characters. *And* enchanted mirrors.

It's probably time to peek in on Ever After, so let's start with…um…*ooh!* I know![19] Inside a particular enchanted mirror, where the Evil Queen is imprisoned. There she is now, dressed in a black, purple, and silver gown topped with a grand headdress, as if she's never heard of *casual wear*. This is the same Evil Queen who poisoned Snow White, but she didn't stop there. After she played her part in that tale, she

---

19 Oops, sorry, I'm not saying *I* anymore. I promise.

got up to a lot more nastiness, trying to take over other people's fairytales and even the entire world of Wonderland. To stop her rampage, Headmaster Grimm and other magically gifted faculty from Ever After High caught her and trapped her in the high-security mirror prison.

Even so, she *has* managed to escape before. Who knows? Maybe she will again, because right now the mirror prison walls are shaking. Just for a second. As if the prison were a cell phone buzzing with a call coming in. Wait. Do they have cell phones in Ever After? Let me check my Narrator Handbook.... Oh yeah, they have *Mirror*Phones. Not sure if those buzz. Maybe a different simile? The walls shook like...like a box of mildly irritated bees? Whatever. The point is, the Evil Queen can feel the shaking.

"*Ooh,*" she says with a smile. "That's promising."

And what is she thinking?[20]

Aha. It seems that she's been enormously, apoc-alyptically bored. Her only entertainment is spying on the people of Ever After through their mirrors. And non-evil people are *so boring*. Besides, what is

---

20 Oh great. I guess I have to peek into that mind of hers and get my evil on.

the point of secretly watching people when you can't, at some point, pop up and shout, *Ha! I have secretly been watching you!*

For the Evil Queen, there is no point. In her opinion, regular people never do anything entertaining on their own. Usually, she has to motivate them with things like pointy sticks, poisoned apples, or abruptly carnivorous plants. But mirror prison dampens the Evil Queen's magic. She can't reach beyond the walls to poke Cinderella with a stick or make Snow White's garden roses hunger for the taste of flesh.

So after all that boring watching, a tiny earthquake is hopeful news.

"But what caused it?" the Evil Queen asks herself.[21] "There's no earth here to shake, so it must be magical. And since I'm the most magical thing around, perhaps it was... me!"

Her smile brightens. The Evil Queen likes to think that she herself is the cause of most interesting things.

"Now..." She taps her chin delicately, aware of

---

21 In my experience, villains either talk to themselves a lot or get a minion they can tell their evil plans to.

how beautiful she is—in a pale, gaudy way. "What was I doing when the tremor happened?"

She was thinking about those little meat-filled dumplings she used to buy from a village shop.[22] She loves those. Maybe dumpling thoughts caused the tremor?

So she begins again to consider dumplings. She thinks so hard about dumplings that she grits her teeth and screams, *"Dumplings! Dumplings! I am thinking about dumplings!"*

But no earthquake.

Her forehead furrows. The lack of dumpling results means something *besides* her probably caused the tremor. What a disappointment.

She puts her black-gloved hand on one of the glass walls of her cell and casts a seeking spell.

Repeal the concealed real.
Reveal the wheel that reeled our keel.

The mirror hums but stays dark.

The Evil Queen removes her glove, slaps her

---

22 Well, mostly she stole them, TBH.

hand to the glass, and shouts, *"Show me what caused the tremor, you insufferable slab of melted sand!"*

The glass wall changes, blurring and fading, light and shadow moving across the pane. She nods in approval. The mirror isn't alive exactly, but everything can benefit from a loud reminder that she is fearsome.

The shadows and light coalesce into the silhouettes of two girls. Strange. She should be able to clearly see anyone in Ever After.[23]

Voices thrum from behind the glass, sound slipping through in pieces.

"...Shadowplopplopplop..."

"Something hap...the map..."

"...Ever After High?"

"Never heard of it..."

"...not Shadow High—"

At the mention of Shadow High, the mirror goes dark, like an eye blinking shut. But those words—*Shadow High*—continue to echo. The Evil Queen's eyes narrow. She prides herself on her ability to

---

23 Maybe that's because the silhouettes aren't of girls in Ever After, but of somewhere far, far away....

notice Powerful Things, and she recognizes power in that name.

"Shadow High," the Evil Queen says, tracing her finger across the dark face of the mirror. Beneath her finger, a tiny spiderweb line of a crack appears. It's no more than an inch long, but it *is* a crack. She can work with cracks. Cracks are how spiders get in. They are how foundations start to crumble.

The Evil Queen starts warming up her most evil, malevolent laugh. Remembering that there is no one there to hear and admire her objectively magnificent laugh, she stops. She keeps smiling, though. Because now she is prepared, and the next time her prison shakes, she will ride that tremor right through the crack in the mirror. Back to Ever After High and her beloved-but-too-good daughter, Raven. And straight to the school's ancient library. The Evil Queen long ago learned that books hold knowledge, and knowledge is power.

Whatever this *Shadow High* is, she smells in its name a power greater than anything she's ever after known.

CHAPTER 5

I T'S MORNING AT EVER AFTER HIGH.[24] THE sunlight cuts through the cotton candy–like clouds, drawing sparkles out of the dew on the humming flowers. Two stray pixies flit past, buzzing about the all-night party at the frog pond. A nearby frog, who apparently wasn't invited to the party, *ribbits* in a way that seems to mean *"Worst. Day. Ever."*

Apple White and Raven Queen, carrying notebooks and hextbooks,[25] are walking past.

---

24 Yes, the same morning I was just telling you about at Monster High. So this stuff was going on around the same time as some of the Frankie and Draculaura stuff. Seriously, it's tricky being a Narrator and jumping around like this!

25 They're like textbooks. It's an Ever After thing.

"Look at that frog!" says Apple. "Doesn't he look so sad?"

"Um, I think 'grumpy' is just resting frog face," says Raven.

"No, no, this frog is especially sad." Apple picks him up, sets him on her palm, and looks deep into his wet eyes. "I don't know what happened to make you so sad, Mr. Frog, but let me assure you that you are a worthy and noble creature and…" She hesitates, flipping her perfectly curled blond hair over her shoulder. "It's not my fairytale to kiss frogs, but just in case…"

Apple puckers her bright-red lips and pecks him on his cold green cheek. He doesn't turn into a prince, but his cold green cheeks do turn warm pink.

"*Ribbit*," he says shyly, and jumps from her hand into the pond to go tell his friends about his Best. Day. Ever.

"Apple White," says Raven as they walk on together, "you are the nicest person I've ever known. How can you still be friends with me when all I do is mess everything up?"

"Raven Queen," says Apple, "you do not mess everything up."

"I can't be evil like my mom," says Raven.[26] "But ever since I refused to become the next Evil Queen, a lot of outrageous stuff has happened. Like, big, bad, dangerous stuff. Crazy stuff."[27]

"And you think it's your fault?" asks Apple.

"Well...maybe? Yeah?" Raven twists a purple lock of hair. "Maybe my choice is a little snowball that keeps rolling till it turns into an avalanche."

"That's too much to put on yourself, Raven."

Raven shrugs. "I just need to hocus focus on my studies, keep my head down, and stay out of trouble."

"Well, I applaud your commitment to your education," says Apple. "See you at lunch!"

Apple continues on toward Princessology 201, held in a glass tower by the sports field, while Raven takes the stairs down to the Dark Sorcery class cellar.

Baba Yaga is sitting cross-legged on her floating stool up in front of the class as Raven drops an apple on her desk and hurriedly takes a seat. Last time she

---

26 In Ever After, all the children of famous fairytale characters are supposed to follow in their parents' footsteps and live out their destined stories. And...I'm trying so hard not to fangirl all over *this* story. *The* Raven Queen! And Apple White! *Sooo* hard to be professional right now, for reals.

27 If you missed this stuff, you can read about it in some books my parents helped narrate.

was late, Baba Yaga turned her into a snail for the entire class period.

The ancient teacher eyes the apple.

"Are you trying to poison me, Ms. Queen?" asks Baba Yaga. Her skin is yellow and thin, wrinkled like old paper, her gray hair long and knotted with strings, shells, bones, and other interesting things.

"What?" Raven says. "No, Madam Baba Yaga, I…I mean, I just thought…"

"Pity," Baba Yaga says with a sigh. "I thought you were finally coming around and embracing your evil."

She opens a desk drawer, knocks the apple into it, and slams it shut. From inside the drawer comes a sound like a dozen ravenous beetles tearing into a meal.

The other students begin to whisper excitedly to one another.

"What was that?"

"I told you she had a pet!"

"Now I know where to put my lunch on days when they serve nine-day-old peas porridge in the Castleteria."

Baba Yaga quiets them with a stare of her ice-blue eyes.

"I found your essays on the practical uses for Dark Magic at unbirthday parties to be *insanely* disappointing," Baba Yaga says in her dry voice. "So today we're going to—"

A tremor rolls beneath their feet. The stone floor and walls of the cellar classroom groan. A great iron cauldron tips over and tumbles down the aisle.

"Whoa!"

"Hey!"

"What in Ever After was that?"

"An earthquake?" says Raven.

Baba Yaga sniffs the air, her nostrils quivering. "I smell…heat. Electricity. And wrongness. Not a normal earthquake." She pulls a knotty stick out of one of her many pockets, waves it in the air, and chants a spell.

Thrown stone tone now be shown.
Spot the birthbomb
that spawned
yon earth moan.

The old sorceress's eyes widen. She gasps. Her lips tremble. And in a raspy whisper, she says, *"What is Shadow High—"* before falling off her stool in a dead faint.

Raven and several other students jump up from their seats. Raven holds the teacher's hand.

"Madam Baba Yaga, are you okay?"

A second tremor rolls through the classroom, knocking over Baba Yaga's collection of glass unicorns. An ogre in the back row yelps with fear.

Raven is just about to go fetch Headmaster Grimm, when suddenly the sorceress opens her eyes.

"What are you doing?" she shouts. "Unhand my hand, Ms. Queen. Everyone, back to your seats, or you'll be spending the rest of the day as invertebrates!"

With a flourish of her arm, she levitates off the floor and onto her stool.

"You fainted … or something," Raven says, hurrying back to her desk. "There was an earthquake and you did a spell to determine its source, but you said 'Shadow High' and then—"

"Shadow High?" says Baba Yaga, her lip curled with disgust. "Never heard of it. Sounds to me like you lot are trying to get out of classwork, hmm? Well, it won't work on me! Open your hextbooks to chapter fifteen and read in silence!"

After an excruciatingly long hour of quiet, the

end-of-class fairybell finally chimes, and Raven speeds out of the cellar room, up into the sparkly, shiny Ever After morning air.

She slips through the crowd of students, keeping an eye out for a mint-green-and-lavender-haired head topped with a teacup hat. She has to tell her BFFA[28] Madeline Hatter about the weird thing with Baba Yaga.

Raven takes three stairs at a time as she climbs. Maddie isn't in her room, but Apple is just coming out of theirs.

"Apple! The weirdest thing just happened—"

"Don't you have Study Ball now?" asks Apple. "Tell me about it while we walk. I don't want to be late to Crownculus class."

"Have you ever heard of something called Shadow High?" asks Raven, walking beside her.

"No," says Apple.

"Did you…er, happen to get mother-goosebumps when I said that name?"

"Actually, I did." Apple rubs her arms. "But

---

28 BFFA=Best Friend Forever After. Madeline Hatter=daughter of the Mad Hatter of Wonderland and just the most *hat-tastic* person ever. Reader, a confession: She is my fave. *Cue fangirl scream.*

probably just because it sounds kind of evil...." Apple shakes her head, as if to clear it. "Whatever-after it is, it sounds like trouble, and just this morning you were determined to stay out of trouble. Try to think about something else. Did Baba Yaga give you a lot of thronework?"

"You're right, you're right," Raven says. She will not let this perfectly normal morning turn into another "adventure" (i.e., "disaster"). Maybe if she just ignores everything—the tremor, Baba Yaga's faint, that old woman there walking down the hall in front of them whose posture reminds her so much of her mother—

"Apple," Raven whispers.

"I get mother-goosebumps all the time," says Apple with forced calmness. "The earthquake was no big deal. Nothing strange is going to happen today. Nothing! We're just—"

"Do you know who that woman is?" asks Raven. "The one whose posture is nearly identical to—"

"Your mom's?" says Apple. "I mean—"

"You think so, too!" says Raven.

"No!" says Apple. "I just...I didn't mean... Study Ball! We've got to get you to Study Ball!"

"But, Apple…what if it *is* her? This wouldn't be the first time my mom broke out of mirror prison and disguised herself. What could she be up to?"

Apple groans. Even her groans sound light and lovely.

"Please," Raven whispers. "If it is my mom and she does something horrible and I don't try to stop her…"

"I guess ignoring a problem won't make it go away, will it?"

Raven hooks Apple's arm in hers, and they rush down the hall just as the woman enters the library. The huge double doors slam shut in their faces.

Raven tries the doors. Locked? In the middle of a school day? It takes her a minute, but at last she manages a spell that unlocks them.

Apple and Raven step into the eight-story library, greeted by silence and the delicious smell of ink and dusty paper. Morning light streaming through the wall of windows gilds the leaves floating softly down from the massive tree pillars. The library is completely empty. Even the Stepsister librarians aren't at the checkout desk. A sign reads:

GONE TO FACULTY MEETING. GO AWAY.

Apple sighs. "See? Nothing fishy going on."

"Yeah…" says Raven. "But that old woman came in, didn't come out, and yet *isn't* here, so that would be—"

"Curious," says Apple. "Mysterious. And possibly magical. As copresident of the Royal Student Council—and your BFFA—I guess it is my duty to help you investigate. But we have to be quick about it! I can do hextra credit for Crownculus, but I cannot miss Kingdom Management. We have finals next week!"

Raven whispers a spell. A ball of glowing blue fog zips around the room, confirming that no one else is here. Still, her gut nags at her, like that sensation she gets after eating peas porridge cold, especially the kind that's in the pot nine days old. She doesn't make a habit of eating it, by the way. Just sometimes it looks weirdly appetizing.

The ball of magic stops at a broken mirror before dissolving into glitter.

"That's weird," says Raven.

"Ugh," Apple murmurs. "I have a fairy bad feeling about this."

"Bad feeling like after eating peas porridge in the pot nine days old?"

"I never eat that stuff!" says Apple. "Well, just the one time. And, to be honest, it wasn't that bad. But *that* is bad," she says, pointing at the broken mirror.

Mirrors are more abundant in Ever After than puddles after a rainstorm. And a broken mirror is always a troubling sign.

But as they get closer, Raven can see it isn't just a mirror. It's a doorway. And through the cracks, she can see an empty room on the other side.

"We probably shouldn't go in," Apple whispers.

"Yeah..." Raven says. "But we probably will."

From somewhere unseen, Raven hears a *plop*... *plop*...

CHAPTER 6

A ROOM HIDDEN BEHIND A MIRROR?" APPLE whispers. "Please let it be nothing at all alarming. Pretty please with an apple on top?"

Raven steps through the jagged hole in the mirror doorway first. It's more of a closet than a room, the walls lined with books so old they are mostly scrolls and parchments.

"A secret book room!" Apple says.

"Who would hide books?" says Raven.

"Someone who didn't want them found," says Apple, hugging her arms around her chest. "Or didn't want them to *escape*."

Raven snorts. It's almost as if Apple thinks the books in the room could be *dangerous*. Books aren't dangerous![29]

Apple points to the floor, where recent footprints disrupt the carpet-like layer of dust.

"She was in here?" says Apple.

"It's like she vanished into thin air," says Raven.

"Or thick air," says Apple, waving away the thick dust from her face.

A single table is covered in dust so heavy it's like moss growing over a fallen log. Two books lie open there, dust-free, as if recently pulled from the shelves. Apple twitches, glancing back at the entrance, then gives up and approaches the books. Raven smiles. There are a few things Apple can't resist: warm apple cobbler with melty ice cream, a parade (any kind—the girl is simply nuts about parades), and books she hasn't read yet.[30]

"She—whoever she is; I'm not convinced she's your mother—but *she* was reading these," says Apple.

---

29 Except when they are!

30 And also—apples.

Raven picks up a scroll, open to a description of something called Monster High.[31]

"Why was my mom reading about campfire stories?" says Raven.

"We don't know it was your—" Apple begins.

"Weird. This talks about an ancient school where mummies and vampires and zombies and other monsters are students, but not as if it's just a story. As if those creatures actually exist."

Apple smooths her perpetually smooth curls. "Headmaster Grimm says it's dangerous to tell made-up stories. He believes we should be focusing on our own stories and achieving our Happily Ever Afters."

"Maybe that's why this book is locked up in here," says Raven. "But why was Mom—"

Apple takes a breath as if about to disagree.

"—or *whoever* it was," Raven amends, "interested in these old stories?"

The second book is more like a pamphlet. Raven picks it up with just her fingertips, afraid that even

31 It's *sooo* weird how we totally know what Monster High is, but they have no idea!

touching the ancient paper will turn it into a pile of dust.

And then, *plop.*

"What's that noise?" asks Apple.

Plop. Plop. Plop.

"I don't know. Maybe leaky pipes. Look, Apple."

Raven holds up the parchment. Most of the words have been erased. Only a few remain, as if whoever erased the other words couldn't quite scrub out the last few: *Shadow High...power...Narrators... the breaking of the world...World of Stories...*

"There's that name again," says Raven.

"You mean Shadow High?" says Apple. She shivers. "I've never heard of a World of Stories before. Sounds like some pretend tale. *Narrators...* Those are the voices Maddie is always talking about, right?"

"Yeah, she says she can hear them speaking," says Raven. "She says Narrators are always telling our story, describing what we're doing and thinking, even."[32]

"Hextremely strange, even for Maddie. But what

32 So awkward when people talk about you like you're not even there. Hello, girls! I'm your Narrator, and I'm right here!

is—there's that plopping sound again! It's fairy distracting! Don't you feel like you want to go figure out where it's coming from?"

"Not really," says Raven. "The castle I grew up in was always full of strange noises. I've learned to ignore them."

At that, the plopping noises die out, like a sad little balloon giving up its last bit of air.

Raven gingerly turns over the parchment, trying to figure out what in Ever After her mother wanted from these books and to anticipate how she might protect her friends from whatever the Evil Queen has in store. She has made that her personal responsibility, but sometimes it feels like trying to stop a tsunami with a tea towel.

"Raven!"

In surprise, Raven nearly drops the paper.

Through the broken mirror bounds Madeline Hatter. Her curls look fluffier than usual; her teacup hat is tipping over one eye; her dress is a dizzying mix of stripes, dots, and assorted prints.

"Raven, you're doing that thing again!"

"Hey, Maddie! Why are you...Uh, what thing am I doing?"

"You know, with the oh-my-golly-pops and heigh-ho-the-dairy-woes, but all wrapped up in a present with a big bow! A purple bow? Is purple your favorite color, Raven? I can't believe I've never asked you that before! Oh! I just realized I walked through a mirror to get here! Am I in Wonderland?"[33]

"Hi, Maddie," says Apple. "We followed a suspicious woman who might be, but not necessarily is, the Evil Queen in disguise into a secret book room that has a hidden mirror door."

"Oh," says Maddie. "So just a typical day, then, huh?"

"Maddie, I'm really glad you're here," says Raven. "Strange stuff is happening. There was that earthquake, and Baba Yaga did a spell and said something about Shadow High—"

"Ah! That's it!" says Maddie. "That's why I came here to talk to you! I'm tickled blue you said that, because I'd already forgotten that they sent me here to this weird little room to tell you about Meadow

---

33 Reader, don't worry if you don't understand everything Maddie says. You wouldn't be the only one.

Fly. Or was it Shallow Pie? *Ooh* yes. Pie. I like pie, don't you?"[34]

"Um, wait," says Raven. "How did you know we were in a secret mirror-doored room in the library, anyway?"

"The Narrators told me, of course!"

Apple and Raven share a look.

"They are so frizzled and froozled and gonk-bonkers today," says Maddie, turning in circles, "like a top spinning on the ceiling and *not* just 'cause it looks fun. The Narrators wanted me to tell you a very important message and made me promise with hooked pinkies and crossed eyes and bendy elbows not to forget."

Maddie smiles up at them. Raven and Apple lean in closer. Maddie smiles bigger, as pleased as a warthog in a mudhole.

"Well?" says Apple. "What's the message?"

"Oh! Right!" Maddie clears her throat. "*STOP.*"

"Stop?"

"Yep. *Stop.* I'm certain they said to tell you to stop. Or was it *hop*? It might have been *hop*. Hopping is

---

34 Yes! Yes, I do!

more fun than stopping, generally, and the Narrators are *soooo* nice I think they'd like us to have fun. Don't you think?"

Maddie starts to hop back through the mirror, then turns as if expecting the two girls to follow. "No hoppity?"

"Maddie," says Raven. "These voices you hear. How did they know about Shadow High?"

Maddie leans in and whispers, "Because they're the *Narrators*. They know almost everything. And they're not supposed to talk to me or any of us, really. So it must be a *big deal* for them to break their super-special rules just to tell me about it. A big, big deal. A big pig-in-a-wig deal."

Raven's mother-goosebumps are back, from her scalp down to her toenails.

In the distance, a fairybell chimes.

Apple groans a delightful groan, sounding almost as light and sweet as a pixie laugh. Raven wonders how she manages it.

"Oh my fairy godmother! We have to leave now for our next class or we'll be late." She takes Raven's and Maddie's arms and walks them out of the library.

Raven looks back over her shoulder as they leave,

scanning the library one more time for any sign of her mother. Now her stomach feels as if it's full of peas porridge *ninety* days old. Something is definitely shadowy. But if Raven gets involved, she worries she'll only make things worse.

CHAPTER 7

AND SO THE THREE GIRLS PART WAYS: APPLE TO Kingdom Management class, Raven to Home Evilnomics, and Maddie to Chemythstry. Rather than taking the stairs, Maddie decides to slide down the banisters all the way to the ground floor, shouting *"whoosh!"* as she goes, because travel is so much more satisfying when it makes a whooshing sound.

You're so right. It is more satisfying! Well done, Narrator.

Oh! Hi, Maddie! I have to say, it's simply bookmarkable that you can hear Narrators. But...er... wow, it's hard to stay professional and not go all italics: *You're THE Madeline Hatter and you're actually talking to me!*

Well, yes, of course I am, sillypants. What else would I be doing, honking to you? It's not even Thursday. Though, really, who says you can only honk on Thursdays?

Um, what?

The Narrators I usually hear are adults, and some are men and some are women, but only you sound like a girl. I suppose you could be an elephant that sounds like a girl. Are you an elephant?

No, I'm—I'm Brooke. Brooke Page.

Brooke! What a tea-lightful name! Like a babbling brook, right? Are you always babbling? Not that I'm one to do the pointing of fingers—

Please babble to me whenever you want. I mean, I know it's against the rules to talk to you, but this is my first big solo narration. I haven't even graduated from Narrator High yet, and I'm only narrating this story because no one else will, and I'm...I'm a little bit scared, Maddie.

Nonsense on toast! Narrators aren't scare-able! Besides, you have me. I'll be right at your side. Or...do you have a side, Brooke?

Sure I do. Sides and top and bottom, too. Feet, head, and hands, just like you. You just can't see me, 'cause Narrators live in a land between the World of Stories and the Fourth Wall, where we can observe all the stories that happen in Ever After and all over the World of Stories, and then we narrate the stories for the Readers who live over the Fourth Wall.[35]

World of what? Fourth, huh? And hey, what's that plopping sound?

Ugh, it's probably my parents. They're using their Plop Device to try to distract you. If I'm not supposed to talk to you at all, then I'm definitely not supposed to be blabbing about secrets like the World of Stories. But they're the ones who keep breaking rules and interfering! I bet they told you to go stop Raven and Apple in the library, didn't they?

---

35 Wow, that was a long sentence! Also, it's okay if you don't know what I'm talking about just yet. Maybe soon I can learn more about the World of Stories and explain it all to you.

If your parents are one womanish and one mannish and both Narratorish, then yes. They were going on and on about Shallow Pie—

Shadow High.

That's it! And they sounded more worried than a giraffe in a rabbit hole.

I guess I should be worried, too, and run as far away from this story as I can get. I'm probably in over my head—

Like a rabbit in a giraffe hole.

But I feel so sure, deep down in my independent clauses, that this story needs to be told. Have you ever felt really, really certain about something?

Absotively. I'm always certain. About everything. There's probably stuff I'd be uncertain about if I saw it, but there's just so much certain stuff going on I forget to notice anything else. And I'm certain about you, Brooke Page. You got this.

Thanks, Maddie.

CHAPTER 8

Let's take a peek at what the Evil Queen is doing now....Aha! Raven was right! That *was* the Evil Queen snooping around Ever After High. We should probably rewind a bit and see what that scoundrel has been up to.

Okay, here she is when she first arrives at Ever After High this morning, not looking at all like the gowned, headdressed monarch we saw in the mirror prison. She's woven an illusion around herself, borrowing the face of an old woman with white hair and soft wrinkled skin. Once before when she escaped mirror prison, she infiltrated Ever After High disguised as a young student, so she went for something quite different this time. The disguise is, she is certain, *exceptional.*

"Of course, everything I do is exceptional," the Evil Queen whispers to herself.[36]

She can't quite force herself to shuffle down the hall looking meek and inconspicuous, though. She is the Evil Queen! She simply must straighten her spine and stretch her legs in long, confident strides. It's all she can do to stop herself from declaring, *I have escaped! I have made it to Ever After High despite everything! I am your queen!*

Instead, she clenches her teeth together, keeping silent. It's *sooo* hard for her.

And then a mass of lavender and mint green tumbles into her path.

"It *is sooo* hard to stay silent, isn't it?" Madeline Hatter says. "I play the quiet game with my pet rock, and little Igneous is *always* beating me."

The disguised queen takes a step back.

"*Oooh*, you're a disguised queen?" Maddie says.

"How... What makes you say that?"

---

36 Not because she hears me. The Evil Queen doesn't even know Narrators exist! Like I said, villains just like to mutter to themselves about how great they are.

"Because I heard the Narrator call you a disguised queen."

"Narrator?"

"Oh, don't be scared! Narrators aren't like alligators, even though they sound the same," Maddie says. "I mean their names, not their voices, because alligators don't talk, especially not on Thursdays, because that's all about honking—"

"I demand to know why these Narrators are talking about me!"

"Oh, it's nothing personal. Narrators talk about everybody and know *everything*. But no one hears them, hexcept me and Kitty Cheshire, though she pretends not to." Maddie is whispering, her hand held to one side of her mouth, as if to prevent her words from escaping.

"Wait, what? Words need to escape?" Maddie shouts at the ceiling. "Aw, poor little words trapped in my mouth! I should help them escape. Be free, little words," she yells, making shooing motions from her mouth. "Be free!"

Maddie cartwheels down the hall, shouting as many words as she can, especially words she hasn't ever said, in case they have been trapped inside her for too long.

"*Amorphous*, be free! *Antediluvian*, your life is your own! *Cyclopean! Eldritch! Fetid! Gibbous!*" she shouts as she tumbles away.

The Evil Queen hurries in the opposite direction. Wonderlandians are generally odd, but that one almost seemed to be reading her mind. The queen makes a mental note to investigate the Hatter child further, and whatever a "Narrator" is, after she pins down this whole "Shadow High" business.

She shuffles into the library. A sleeping spell tingles on the tips of her fingers, ready to zap at anyone who might be in the library, but the room is empty.

"Fools," the Evil Queen mutters. "This room should be constantly crowded with students eager for knowledge. Don't they know what power hides between book covers?"

That the students are all fools is no surprise to her. She *was* hoping to find her daughter in the library, but perhaps it's just as well. Raven would only try to stop her. She casts a spell to lock the library doors, and then undoes her disguise spell by reaching up, grabbing something unseen, and making an unzip-ping motion.

"Now then," she says, shaking out her purple skirt and straightening her impressive headdress. "Time to get to work."

She casts a seeking spell for books on Shadow High, but the closest thing she finds is a collection of essays on the height of shadows at various times of the day. After throwing that book on the ground and kicking it for good measure, she tries a different spell.

Seek now the hidden,

Not a certain edition, not that

shadow unbidden.

Seek the cage of the strange, the

shelves with the mange

Where the dangerous tomes call home.

Purple fog coalesces into a kind of snake that slithers through the air. The Evil Queen follows it as it darts through the shelves of the library, around corners, and up stairs, and then finally crashes into a mirror mounted on the wall.

She makes a fist, orange energy crackling around her hand, and punches. A wave of force pulses from her fist, and the mirror shatters. Behind the mirror is not a wall but a room.

"Mirror prisons for dangerous people, mirror prisons for dangerous books," the Evil Queen says, stepping through the crack.

The shelves are labeled, and one brass plaque reads HISTORIES. In any Ever After library, Histories is the section where you find the fairytales of Ever After: the true stories of Cinderella, Snow White, Sleeping Beauty, and so on.

But the Histories shelf here is filled with campfire tales—stories about people who Raven, Apple, and everyone else in Ever After are certain *aren't* real. Dracula. Frankenstein. Boogey Men. Monster stories that parents in Ever After tell their children to frighten them into behaving. Headmaster Grimm forbids writing down stories about monsters. Yet here they are, fully bound, as if Dracula is just as real as Prince Charming.

"Strange," mutters the Evil Queen.

She magically speed-reads all the books in Histories, then moves deeper into the Nonfiction shelf. There she finds a stack of old Ever After High school records. A parchment *yawn*ingly titled *Yearly Attendance Across Districts* features a list of schools. Ever After High is there, as is Wonderland High. Shadow High is not. But there are others. Many others. Some she has heard about.[37] Most she has not.[38] How could there be so many schools she's never heard of? She is supposed to know everything! Are they ancient, defunct schools?

She casts a sensing spell and draws her finger down the list. *Ever After High* gives a pulse, as she expected. *Wonderland High* twitches, which confirms that it still exists. And then on *Monster High*, her finger visibly sparks. She pulls her hand back, blowing away smoke that trails from her glove.

"Well, hello there," she says.[39] "Monster High, is it? That sounds dark and mysterious. Perhaps it's

---

37 Like Faerie Highe. Faerie was on the Evil Queen's Places to Invade After I Conquer Wonderland list, but when she discovered the fairies spent much of their time throwing digested glitter at one another, she decided not to bother.

38 Like Mr. Aardvark's Academy for Anthropomorphic Anteaters in Fun Fauna Land, which I think closed down shortly after the Great Insect Uprising.

39 I startle every time she talks to herself, because for a second I think she's talking to me.

even an alternate name for Shadow High. And judging by that spark, someone at this very moment must be looking for a way out. I think I should pay this place a visit. Best to strike while the iron is hot, as they say.[40] I'm afraid you've hidden from me far too long, my evil little friends."

Weaving magic about herself, the queen chants.

Hook this High
where monsters lie,
crook that nook of land,
find the sand
of the beach
where creatures reach
to seek a peek
inside
Ever After-wide.

---

40 I'm not sure who says that. Laundry workers? Blacksmiths, maybe? I think her point is that because Frankie and Drac are looking for Ever After High at the same time she is looking for Monster High, the magic crosses and therefore paves an easier path to move from one to the other?

A swirling vortex of magical energy appears above the Evil Queen's head. She rotates her hand in time with the motion of the vortex.

Hang my tether on
open weather,
bolt this shock to the dock
on the edge of that notional ocean,
and plant me on this land
in the lee of an unseen sea.

She flexes her hand, and a bolt of lightning strikes the swirling green mass. The library around her vanishes, and she is moving through a whitewash fog of nothing. Two shadows flick past her in the mist. Finally her boots touch earth.

She is standing before an ancient house, dark and sinister. It is as if someone had tried to re-create her castle of power from the old days but neglected to include the moat and all the delightful death traps. She hears voices and…howling?…from inside, and she enters through the front doors.

Before her are gathered a most beautiful collection of malevolent beasts. There are wolf creatures, semitransparent fiends, and the animated skeletons of the dead. There is an incomprehensible gelatinous mass, eyes floating loose in its body. The Evil Queen smiles, raising her arms to the gathered group.

"Children of darkness! I am here to lead you!" She clenches her fists, meaning to invoke a spell that will make her glow, but nothing happens. The effort to send herself to Monster High has temporarily drained her of power. "I am here to drive you to your destinies of power!" she continues, certain her words alone will be impressive enough. "With me at your head, there will be nothing to stop us! The weak of the world will scream in terror at our advance! They will bend their knees to us or be destroyed!"

The Evil Queen's voice booms as if she were the thunder itself.

The gathered students of Monster High stare. Some shift. Deuce Gorgon, son of Medusa, unsuccessfully tries not to laugh.

"Is that the new Hagriculture teacher?" whispers Cleo de Nile.

"I have no idea," Clawdeen Wolf replies. "But let's get out of here before she starts yelling again."

"Good idea," says Cleo.

"Hey, have you seen Drac and Frankie?" Clawdeen asks as they walk away to class.

CHAPTER 9

OKAY, SO I'M PRETTY SURE THOSE TWO SHADOWS the Evil Queen passed in the mist on her way to Monster High were Frankie and Draculaura. But how did that happen? We'd better jump back an hour. Again. Last time—I promise![41]

Oh look, Frankie is on the roof of Monster High. She isn't usually afraid of heights, but the roof of Monster High is all turrets and towers and spires, which look great from a distance, but when you are trying to climb them in lace-up platform wedges, it's

---

[41] Not saying *I* anymore. Nope. Not gonna do it. Totally a professional Narrator, thank you very much.

less "My, but isn't that interesting architecture?" and more *"AAAHHH!!!"*[42]

She's just attached a thick cable to a lightning rod atop the east tower when she slips. "Wha… wha… *whoaaa*!" she yells.

She grabs the cable to slow her slide and comes to a squeaking halt at the point where roof meets sky and fifteen meters of nothing open up below her.

The seams on her left wrist pop, and her hand continues down without her.

"No!" she yells.

But just then a bat streaks out an open window and catches the hand. The bat dips down a bit with the weight of the hand, but keeps flying; then it wheels around and goes back inside.

Frankie drops onto a ledge and slides in through the open window of the Mad Science lab just in time to see the bat embiggen back into Draculaura.

"Here, you dropped this," says Draculaura, tossing the hand.

"Thanks," says Frankie. "As your dad would say,

---

42 Sorry, Reader. That sentence was a little long.

you really took me by the hand. I've got to hand it to you, Drac. You had the upper hand, but, you know, even without my left hand, I was all right—"

Draculaura tosses a pillow at her.[43] "What were you doing up there, anyway? Why'd you want to meet me in here?"

"To help figure out this Ever After thing," Frankie says.

"By roof jumping?"

"Ha! *Not* my plan," Frankie says. "I want to enhance the Mapalogue."

Frankie leans out the window. No cable in sight. She places her detached hand on the bricks and watches it climb back up the wall like a spider. As soon as it's out of sight, she closes her eyes to concentrate, feeling her hand reach the edge of the roof and climb up. This is the trick with controlling body parts that aren't attached to you—unless they are eyeballs. Then you can't see what you are doing.

At last, Frankie senses the long, smooth bump of the cable and has her hand grab hold and leap

---

43 Weird—why is there a pillow in the Mad Science lab?

over the edge. Through the window, Frankie catches it with her other hand and pulls in both hand and cable.

"This is an electrical cable," she says, stitching her hand back on and then deftly peeling individual strands of wire from the cable bundle. "And the other end is connected to the lightning rod on the roof."

Draculaura gestures to an outlet on the wall of the Mad Science lab. "We do have normal electricity."

Frankie glances sidelong at the outlets. "I don't trust them. The power is dodgy—the voltage is too low. Besides, lightning is more reliable—at least if you're me and you can feel when it's coming. Which is"—Frankie tastes the air, examines the little hairs on her arms, and sniffs—"in ninety seconds."

"I brought the Mapalogue, like you asked," says Draculaura. "I set it on that metal table thingy dangling by chains from the ceiling."

"The It's-Alive-o-Tron?" Frankie says.

"That's what that table is called?" Drac asks, taking a step back. "'The Saliva-Tron'? Gross. Is there spit on it?"

"The *It's. Alive. O. Tron*," Frankie says, clamping the cable to the Mapalogue.

"I'm kidding," Draculaura says, putting an arm around Frankie's shoulders. "Sorry, I'm teasing. I'm just…"

She shrugs, but Frankie can read the expression without any words. Draculaura is joking around because she feels nervous. Scared about whatever Frankie is going to do. Frankie straightens, determination heating her bones, warming her muscles. She will *not* let Draculaura down.

"So the lightning should, like, jump-start the Mapalogue with a jolt of electricity," says Frankie. "I'm hoping that with more power we can get it to expand the area where it works and find this Ever After High." She licks her finger and holds it up as if checking for a breeze. "Fifteen seconds."

The girls hold the Skullette and look at the spot on the map that says EVER AFTER HIGH.

"Just like before?" Draculaura asks.

"Just like before," Frankie says. "But this time, with lightning."

"*Exsto monstrum the principal of Ever After High.*" They speak the commanding words just as lightning strikes. The electricity shoots through the cable, into the Mapalogue, up to the Skullette, and into the girls. They buzz with shock, the Skullette sparks, and the Mapalogue glows.

"*Aaaah!*" says Drac, her pink-streaked black hair standing two feet up from her head.

"Hold on!" says Frankie.

A shudder, a *whoosh*, and they're shooting through darkness. Frankie feels as if someone has grabbed her by her stomach and yanked her forward, the rest of her body following a second later. Her limbs vibrate, and her head leans back as if she's moving at an incredible speed, but she can see nothing until a shadow, sparking with black-and-green energy, flits across her vision.[44]

As suddenly as the Mad Science lab around them vanishes, it is replaced by a view of a beautiful fountain of crystal-clear water, a shining fairytale castle behind it. Frankie and Draculaura clatter to the cobblestoned ground. Frankie looks up into an unfamiliar face.

It belongs to a tall, round-bellied man with gray hair, a fancy blue suit, and a mustache that

---

44 The Evil Queen! That was totally the Evil Queen!

doesn't quite meet in the middle. Milton Grimm, the headmaster of Ever After High, is staring at Frankie and Draculaura as if they have popped out of thin air. Which, Frankie supposes, they probably have.

CHAPTER 10

"ELLO!" FRANKIE SAYS, WAVING. SHE IS DOING her best to be exceptionally cheerful, because she knows how she would feel if a couple of people popped out of thin air in front of her. Well, actually, she herself would probably be excited to meet the popper-inners and would ask a lot of questions. But Headmaster Grimm looks how Frankie imagines *Normies* would react if a monster suddenly appeared in front of them.

Frankie figures it's best to be exceptionally friendly. So friendly, in fact, that she waves a little too vigorously and her hastily reattached hand pops off at the seams and tumbles to the ground. The headmaster's eyes widen in horror.

"Oops," Frankie says. "Sorry." She nods at her detached hand, and it scampers back to her like a frightened pet.

Headmaster Grimm's mouth drops open, and Frankie is pretty sure he is about to scream, but someone beats him to it.

"*eeeeee!*" screeches a high-pitched voice. A tiny girl, no bigger than a thumb, is standing on a flower by Frankie's feet.

"*monsters! monsters!*" the tiny girl screams.

"Monsters?" someone asks from the small crowd that's gathering. Everyone looks Normie normal, except for wearing sort of fancy clothes. Have they interrupted some kind of Normie festival or outdoor play?

"Monsters?" Headmaster Grimm repeats. He laughs uneasily. "There's no such thing as monsters."

"Well, um…" Draculaura says, smiling big and doing her best to look friendly.

"Look at her teeth!" someone shouts. "She has *fangs*!"

"Ooh!" Draculaura pops into bat form. "Oops,"

Bat-Drac squeaks, back into girl form. "Sorry. When I get spooked, sometimes I—"

"*Vampire!*"

"There…there's…*ahem*…no such thing as vampires," Headmaster Grimm says, all color draining from his face. "Go to class now, students."

"And that—that *thing*!"

At the word *thing*, Frankie fumbles her hand, and it drops back to the ground.

"*And* there's no such *thing* as…as whatever that is," Headmaster Grimm says, frowning at Frankie as she scrambles to pick up her severed hand.

Several people are still screaming, but many have moved on to angry muttering.

"I've read stories about this," whispers Draculaura. "When Normies go from screaming to muttering, pitchforks and torches are next. We should run."

"Run where? Where are we?"

"I don't know," Draculaura says. "A Normie city?"

"But something's off," says Frankie. "They aren't dressed like any Normies I've seen. And that one girl is, like, two inches tall."

"Well, they aren't monsters—that's for sure," Draculaura says. "Maybe we're in France."

"*Did I hear someone cry 'monster'?*" calls out a guy about their age who is framed in the doorway of the school. He is tall and athletic looking, with perfectly styled golden hair.

"He seems nice," Draculaura whispers.

The boy hurriedly unzips his backpack and draws out a gleaming sword. "*Present yourself for slaying, foul monster!*"

"I take it back," Drac says. "Not nice. Not nice at all. Back to the running plan."

"There's a forest that way," Frankie says, nodding in the direction of a dark wood that seems the best possible option for a monster habitat.

"Right," says Drac. "Run."

They take off at a sprint. Behind them they hear Headmaster Grimm yell, "Mr. Charming! No slaying on school property! Put that sword away right now!"

Frankie runs so hard she nearly bursts at the seams, her jumping gallop trying to keep pace with Draculaura's speedy gait.

The two girls skid to a stop at the edge of the forest.

"They aren't chasing," Frankie says. "Should we—?"

"Go back home?" Draculaura says. "Yes, please. It's too bright with the sun and too sparkly with the clothes and too sharp with the swords. I don't know what this Ever After even is."

A crash sounds from within the forest.

"Is that a good noise or a bad noise?" Frankie asks.

"I've got the Skullette," Draculaura says. "We can go back."

"Okay," Frankie says, looking toward the forest sound, "but we worked so hard to get here. We should try to investigate, at least. Maybe that's a friendly…er…mob?"

"Let's not risk it."

"You're right."

They both grab the Skullette and shout *"Exsto monstrum Dracula!"*

Nothing happens. Certainly not the thrust back home to Draculaura's dad that they were expecting.

"The Skullette isn't humming," Frankie says. "Doesn't it usually output a little energy when we hold it?"

The crashing noise is getting louder. Whatever it is will be upon them soon.

"Let's try someone else's name," Draculaura says. "Ready? One, two…"

"*Exsto monstrum Clawdeen Wolf!*" they shout.

And nothing happens. Again.

A hooded girl leaps from the woods at a dead run. The monster girls scream.[45]

"Hey, it's okay. Calm down," the hooded girl says. "You're scaring people."

"*We're* scaring people?" Draculaura says. "*You're* the one who just leaped at us from a dark forest!"

"Sorry," Cerise says. "I wasn't trying to scare you. I just wanted to catch up to you before Headmaster Grimm did."

"Are you one of them?" Frankie asks. "One of those Normies who were just a hop and a skip from pitchforks and torches?"

The girl removes her hood and smiles. Her teeth are sharp. Pointed ears tipped with tufts of fur poke out from underneath her hair, and her eyes flash yellow.

"I don't know what Normies are," says Cerise, "but I don't think I am one."

---

45 Only because they don't know this is the friendly Cerise Hood, daughter of Little Red Riding Hood and the Big Bad Wolf.

"At last!" Drac relaxes. "A monster! Hey, do you know Clawdeen Wolf?"

"Yeah, is she your cousin, maybe?" says Frankie. "She's a werewolf, too."

"I don't know who Clawdeen is," Cerise says, looking around nervously. "And I'm not a werewolf. Werewolves are monsters, and monsters aren't real—" She gives the two monsters a once-over and shakes her head. "That is...I don't know what's real. Don't tell anyone else about my ears, okay? I just wanted you to know that you're not alone. Don't worry. Ever After isn't *that* weird."

Just then a giant chicken leaps out of the forest.

At least, Frankie thinks it is a giant chicken at first. It has giant chicken legs. But instead of a giant chicken body, there is a cottage, like the kind an old-school witch might live in.

"I'd better go," says Cerise, pulling on her hood and slipping into the shadows. "But don't worry. You'll be okay!"

A woman who looks remarkably witchy herself perches on the roof. The witch cackles, and Frankie relaxes. Witches feel closer to monster than Normie.

Baba Yaga's chicken-legged hut struts toward the girls and squats to ground level.

"That is a fangtastic house, ma'am!" Draculaura calls up to Baba Yaga. "Where did you get it?"

The door to the hut swings open, and Headmaster Grimm steps out.

"We need to get you safely back to my office, um… girls," Headmaster Grimm says. "Into Madam Baba Yaga's hut now. Try not to be scared of it."

"Scared?" Draculaura says, leaping into the hut. "This thing is clawesome!"

The floor of the hut sways as it stands on its chicken legs and begins to walk.

Draculaura looks out the window. "I *so* want one of these chicken houses!"

Baba Yaga sniffs. "This one is mine. You can't have it."

"No, of course not. But wait, you said 'this one.' Are there more of these somewhere?"

"No," Baba Yaga says. "Maybe. Which is to say, I am done talking about chicken huts."

The hut makes its way across the campus, stopping just outside the window of Headmaster Grimm's office on an upper floor of the building. The hut stands on its clawed toes, its front door opening and lining up with the office window. The foursome climbs through the window into the headmaster's grand, book-filled office.

"What are you hexactly?" Baba Yaga asks, poking at Frankie. "Flesh golem? Reanimated corpse? Zombie? Homunculus?"

"Don't be ridiculous," says Headmaster Grimm. "None of those things exist!"

"I…I'm Frankie," she says. "Frankie Stein. My father, Frankenstein, made me in his laboratory."

The color drains from Headmaster Grimm's face. "That's preposterous!"

"With what did your father make you? Sugar? Spice? Clay, maybe?" Baba Yaga pinches Frankie's arm. "Doesn't feel like clay…."

"I'm not sure," Frankie says. "With different pieces. Sewn together."

"Different pieces of *what*?" Baba Yaga asks, one eyebrow arching.

"This is all nonsense," Headmaster Grimm says. "Frankenstein is a character in a campfire tale, a *non*-story that is, I might add, forbidden!"

Baba Yaga shrugs. "Flesh golem, then," she mutters.

Headmaster Grimm ignores the witch. "I don't allow students to tell monster stories," he continues. "It makes for sleepless nights, provokes dark ideas, and interferes with Happily Ever Afters. You two will need to stay hidden away here. You've already done too much damage."

Frankie looks around the office. "We have to stay ... here? In this room? For how long?"

"Until we can figure out who you really are and what to do with you!"

The headmaster and the witch leave the office. The dead bolt slides into place, locking them in.

"I'm sorry, Drac," says Frankie. "I'm so sorry. This is one hundred percent my fault."

"No, it's okay," says Draculaura, but she sits in the corner, curled up, her arms around her knees, and nothing about her looks remotely okay.

CHAPTER 11

RAVEN: Hey Mad where are you?

MADDIE: In Headmaster Grimm's office
guarding monsters

RAVEN: Um what?

MADDIE: Headmaster Grimm asked Apple to
watch the monsters and Apple asked me to
help cuz we're the copresidents of the royal
student council. He and the other teachers
are off having the talkytalk biz. They're all
what do we do I don't know there's monsters
in Ever After aah run away. Like that.

RAVEN: When you say monsters what do you mean?

MADDIE: Monsters. Rawr. AAH! You know like the stories. You should come I've never met monsters before so cool. Only don't try to come through the door its locked, no matter how much I sing at it and feed it noodles

To get in through the upper-story window, Raven hitches a ride on the back of her pet dragon.[46]

"Thanks, Nevermore," says Raven. "Can you get any closer?"

The huge purple dragon hovers outside the office window, inching close enough that her head nearly touches the glass. Raven runs down her pet's back and onto her head and leaps to the window ledge. She clings to the stones with one hand and knocks frantically.

Maddie opens the window and smiles. "Raven! Come in! This is like a holiday. There should be a We Just Met Monsters Day! We could eat creepy foods and have a dance party in a swamp. Or just a

46 If I had a pet dragon, I'd pretty much always be hitching rides on it.

tea party, maybe. Really, a tea party works for any occasion."

"I'm royally glad you're here, Raven," Apple says as Raven hops down into the room. Apple has on her plastered smile, the smile that means, "I'm trying to be cool but really I'm flipping out." Her grin gets even larger and she adds, "Meet our... *guests,* Frankie Stein and Draculaura."

In the corner, two figures stand with their backs against the wall, their faces in shadow.

"Hey, hi, I'm Raven. Raven Queen. Nice to meet you?"

The girls take a couple of tentative steps closer. The light catches their faces. A green-skinned face with one green eye and one blue, stitches around her neck holding on her head. The other pale as the moon, with canine teeth as long as... as long as a...

"*Whoa!*" says Raven, taking a step back. "Sorry. Sorry, I just didn't hexpect you. You're like characters out of a story."

Apple's smile stiffens, and she says without moving her lips, "They're monsters, Raven. Real. Live. Monsters. Isn't that just... just hexcellent?"

Raven has seen griffins, cockatrices, basilisks,

and even the Jabberwock. Some people call trolls and dragons *monsters*, and they are all over Ever After. But dragons and griffins and trolls and such are *real*. These girls are make-believe things who walked straight out of a scary story. Raven's head feels as light as a charmflower seed puff.

"Are…are you…?" Draculaura says, squinting at Raven.

Raven feels a bead of sweat roll down her back, but to keep herself from running away, she takes a cue from Apple and slaps on what she hopes is a comforting smile. Her smile reveals her perfectly normal teeth.

Draculaura sighs with disappointment. "Oh… never mind. I guess not…I just thought…I thought you were like me."

Raven swallows. Her first day at Ever After High, she couldn't take a couple of steps out of her room without someone screaming in terror and running away from the Evil Queen's daughter. "Um, maybe I am," she says. "What are you like? Lost? I've felt lost before."

"No, no, I mean, you know, I'm a *vampire*."

"You're a…"

Draculaura folds her arms. "Fair warning: If you

know what's good for you, don't try to stick me in a coffin."

"What? No way!" Raven exclaims. "Do you know how cool it is to be mistaken for a vampire? Only slightly less cool than actually meeting one."

"Really?" Draculaura smiles.

"Vampires aren't real," Apple says through clenched teeth.

"I know!" Raven laughs. "That's what makes this so fableous. So, Draculaura, can you turn into a bat?"

"Sure."

"So. Cool," Raven says. "I met all kinds of creatures in my mom's castle when I was a kid, but I thought straight-up bat-vampires were just stories."

Apple takes a step backward. "Oh! Do you… er…eat…um, red meat?"

"No," says Draculaura. "But my dad does."

Apple gasps.

"But he's trying to quit!" says Draculaura. "Really! It would be much healthier for him if he were vegetarian like me.…"

"A vegetarian vampire?" Raven rubs her hands together with delight. Tiny bits of purple magic spark into the air. "And you?"

Frankie clears her throat and looks back at the dark corner as if wishing she could hunker down there longer, but she says, "I was made. Stitched together in a laboratory. My dad is Frankenstein."

"No," says Apple, finally unfreezing her smile. "This. Isn't. Possible. That is a character in a campfire story. Frankenstein isn't real."

"Well, *we're* kinda characters in stories," says Raven.

"But *we* are not make-believe!" says Apple. "We inherit stories. Just because my mother is Snow White—"

"Waitwaitwait," says Frankie. "Your mother is *Snow White*? Like in the Normie fairytale? Poisoned-apple, friendly-with-dwarfs *Snow White*?"

Apple sniffs. "They prefer *dwarves* with a *v*, but yes."

"That's impossible," says Frankie. "That's just a story."

"*Just* a story?" says Apple. "Like you're *just* alive?"

"What I mean is, that can't be true," says Frankie. "Snow White isn't a real person."

Apple pulls out her MirrorPhone. "I assure you she is. I could call her for you if you want."

"It just doesn't make any sense," Frankie says.

"Well," Draculaura says, "there *is* precedent. Normies don't think my dad is real. Or your dad. Or Clawdeen's mom. Or us, either, really. But we are. They are. Maybe this is the same kind of thing."

"*We're* the Normies in this situation?" says Frankie.

Draculaura shrugs. "Maybe."

"Anyone else feel like the whole world's been turned upside down?" asks Raven.

Apple, Draculaura, and Frankie all raise a hand.

Frankie's hand falls off. Apple shrieks.

"My dad is the *Mad Hatter of Wonderland*!" Maddie yells from atop a chair.

"Of course he is," Frankie says, getting out a needle and thread for the umpteenth time today. "And your mom is probably the Cheshire Cat."

"Well, not hexactly. She's Kitty's mom!"

"Right," Frankie says, turning to Raven. "So who's your mother?"

"That's... a long story."

"The Evil Queen!" Maddie says helpfully. "The Greatest Evil Ever After Has Ever Known."

Raven notices that the chair Maddie is standing on is one of five around a table set with teacups, saucers, a steaming teapot, and plates of sandwiches that most definitely weren't there a few minutes before.

"Whoa, Maddie, where did you get a tea party?"

Maddie laughs so hard she falls to the floor, holding her belly and rolling around. She can barely speak through the laughs. "'Maddie…where did you get…a tea party'…so funny…best joke ever…'"

Half an hour later,[47] everyone is sitting around the table, drinking cups of fairy blossom tea and chatting. They've gotten past the "Wait, fairytales are *real*?" and "Wait, monster stories are *real*?" parts of the conversation and are trying to understand how they can be from different worlds that somehow don't connect.

"Hexcept through magic," says Raven.

"Yes, that's right!" says Draculaura. "Whatever force pulled us here, it smelled like magic."

"I didn't notice any smell," says Frankie.

---

47 Sorry, I had to take a snack break.

"I smell it whenever I turn into a bat," says Drac. "It's like after-rain—"

"But also a little, um, tangy?" says Raven.

"Exactly! Like tangy after-rain smell," says Drac, "but with, like, sprinkles of something sweet—"

"Kinda like a baking cake—"

"Yeah, like a fruity-flavored cake that's baking in a tangy after-rain oven."

"Hexactly!"

Raven and Draculaura laugh at the same time.

Also at the same time, Frankie and Apple reach for a crustless cucumber sandwich. Their hands bump.

"Sorry," Apple whispers back, pulling her hand away quickly. She's afraid of making Frankie's hand pop off again.

"It's okay," Frankie whispers back, pulling her own hand away just as quickly.

They don't make eye contact.[48]

"Oh wait," says Raven, her laugh dying. "If magic pulled you here, then…Oh curses, maybe it was my—"

---

48 Awkward!

"We don't know it's her, Raven," says Apple.

"That woman was in the library, she did some spell, and then she was gone. What if it was my mom? Where'd she go?"

"You think she switched places with us?" says Draculaura. "What would your mom do if she got to Monster High?"

"Wait, you're from Monster High?" asks Raven. "Yeah, okay, that makes sense, 'cause she was reading about it just before she disappeared—"

"She's in mirror prison, Raven," says Apple.

"Okay, okay." Raven sighs. "I know I'm not supposed to do this, but . . . I just need to be sure. Apple, would you mind helping me?"

They plod over to Grimm's standing mirror. Raven chants a spell, and Apple hacks into the Mirror Network. Once past the security, Raven swipes at the glass and connects to the mirror where her mother is supposedly imprisoned. But the cell is empty.

Raven sits on a chair, her head in her hands. "I'm so sorry."

"Is it bad that the mirror isn't working?" Draculaura says. "I totes can't see my reflection, either. Putting on mascara is tricky, let me tell you."

"Raven wasn't trying to see her own reflection in the mirror," Apple says. "She was trying to see her mother."

"It's my fault," Raven says.

Maddie examines a sandwich. "No, I don't think so. How could it be your fault that the sandwiches taste like the inside of a hat, Raven? It's science. When a sandwich sits in a hat for any number of hours, it will naturally absorb the surrounding hatness—"

"No, I mean that Draculaura and Frankie are stuck in Ever After," says Raven. "It's my mom. I know it. She did this. I ignored it. I didn't stop her."

"Stuck?" says Frankie. "There must be a way to get home."

"You're stories to us," says Apple. "Stories in a book. There's no Monster High in Ever After."

"Or in Wonderland, either," says Maddie with a heavy sigh. "Such a shame. Monsters always make things more interesting."

"We can't find your home on a map," says Apple. "It's not like you could just walk there. How can we help you get back? How is it even possible that there are multiple worlds at all?"

Raven's stomach hurts. And it's probably not from

the hat-flavored sandwiches.[49] When she thought she saw her mother, she should have gone straight to Headmaster Grimm, even if he hasn't exactly been on Team Raven lately. Even if he might not have believed her. She should have risked it in order to stop her mom. And now these girls are far from home and stuck, perhaps, forever after.

49 Not completely, anyway.

CHAPTER 12

THE EVIL QUEEN STANDS IN THE DARK FRONT hall of Monster High, her gown impressively spiky, her headdress magnificently spooky, her wicked hands held out in a most commanding way. Her voice booms.

"Monsters! Heed me, your ruler, your mentor, your queen! Stand and quake in my terrible presence!"

"Um…" says Woolee, twisting a lock of her long fur. "What does *mentor* mean? Isn't that a kind of candy?"

Her friend Gob whispers loudly, "So she wants us to eat her? Seems a bit much."

"Sorry, lady," says Deuce Gorgon, walking past her. "No offense, but I can't be late for Casketball practice."

"No," the Evil Queen says, positioning her fingers in just the right way for a mind-control spell. "What you need is...*to do my bidding*!"

The snakes coiling in a Mohawk out of Deuce's head roll their eyes at the Evil Queen.

"Whatever, dude," Deuce says.

"*Hssss*," say his snakes.

"*You!*" the Evil Queen shouts, pointing at Bonesy. "*Skeleton thing! Come hither!*"

Bonesy shakes his head with a dry rattling sound. He holds up a skeletal arm in a talk-to-the-hand gesture and keeps walking.

"This is absurd!" she says. "*You are creatures of terror!* You are monsters! How dare you disobey me?"

The front hall empties until only the large purple transparent blob of a goblin is left. Gob smiles at the Evil Queen, opens something that might be a mouth, and burps.

"That is just repulsive," says the Evil Queen.

Gob laughs and then shambles down a coffin-lined hallway, making a *shlump-gwee* noise as he goes.

The Evil Queen grumbles. "This is clearly not Shadow High."

"What is this...Shadow High you speak of?" asks Moanica D'kay from behind her. Her voice has a roughness to it, as if she's just awoken from a very long nap.

The Evil Queen whirls. She is not accustomed to being surprised.

Moanica walks slowly up a staircase. Her skin is gray, her arms akimbo as if she is about to strike a pose. Purple hair streaked with yellow-green adds to her sallow complexion, and the Evil Queen is certain that she's not currently alive—not in the traditional sense. Movement behind her gives the impression that there are more *things* in the shadows.

The Evil Queen casts a necromancy spell. "*Corpse Girl,*" she calls. "To my side!"

Someone behind her yelps, but the girl herself just smiles.

"I prefer to be called Moanica," she says. "And whatever spell you're casting, it isn't going to work on me."

The Evil Queen reaches out a hand and, with visible effort, clenches it and pulls it back. As she does, a teenage zombie boy stumbles out of the shadows and shuffles helplessly toward the Evil Queen.

"No?" the Evil Queen says. "My power may be diminished, but it is far from gone."

"Zomboy! Stop!" Moanica shouts.

"Nevertheless," the Evil Queen says, snapping her fingers. The Zomboy falls to the ground, looking dizzy. "It appears taking over this world would be pointless. It isn't what I'm looking for."

"Taking over...?" Moanica shoves the rising Zomboy behind her. "What *are* you looking for?"

"Oh, world domination," says the Evil Queen, examining her fingernails. "Control put back into the hands of those who aren't afraid to wield the power of evil over milquetoast do-gooders—that sort of thing."

Moanica's smile seems real for the first time. "You know, spiky-hat lady, I think we can help each other out. What do you need?"

"Books," says the Evil Queen.

So while everyone else is in class, Moanica sneaks the Evil Queen into Dracula's office. Moanica sniffs and tiptoes around. The Evil Queen runs a fingertip over a massive oak desk, inspecting it for dust.

"Dracula is teaching now, so we have a few minutes," whispers Moanica.

"The *vampire* Dracula?" the Evil Queen says, one thin eyebrow raised in a perfect arch.

"Yes!" Moanica hisses. "I don't know what it's like where you're from, but in this world you need to be *quiet* when you're sneaking."

The Evil Queen's eyes flash red at the insolence of the girl. That this lesser creature would give her orders makes her grind her teeth.

"Ah," the Evil Queen says, understanding. "You are afraid."

"Yes, because we're not supposed to be here."

"But what could you, a zombie, possibly fear?"

"Well, the guy who owns this library, for one," Moanica says.

"Yes, of course. Dracula. The lord of this realm. Surely he would rend you limb from limb for invading his sanctum sanctorum."

"His...um...what? Er...no, he'd probably expel me from school, though," Moanica says. "And that would mess up all my plans!"

"Expel…?" The Evil Queen resists an urge to clap a hand over her face in frustration.

"I don't see any alarms or traps or anything," Moanica whispers. "So look around, but hurry!"

Hurry? The Greatest Evil Ever After Has Ever Known doesn't jump to anyone else's clock, thank you very much! But the process does go much more slowly than she'd prefer. Unable to magically absorb the knowledge in the room, she instead must flip through each book one by one.

Moanica peeks out the office door at her posse of Zomboyz she left as guards.

"For the love of decomposition…Dracula is coming. We've got to get out of here!"

"Go distract him," says the Evil Queen.

A voice echoes from the hall. "Zomboyz, I didn't see you in class today! Did you wish to speak with me about anything?"

"Too late," whispers Moanica. "What if he comes in? We need to hide!"

The Evil Queen casts a cloaking spell, but her choked magic creates an actual cloak that settles on her shoulders.

"I may not be a zombie," Dracula is saying, "but

I am interested in your *brains*. You might even say *dead*icated. Get it?"

The Evil Queen repeats the spell. The cloak changes from red to gray. *So. Irritating!*

"Over here," whispers Moanica. She pulls out a bookcase and stuffs herself behind it.

"*Hmph,*" says the Evil Queen. The space is too narrow for her awesome spiky shoulder pads, but she squeezes in as best she can.

The door opens. "Draculaura, are you in here?" Dracula's voice calls. If he looks too closely, he will discover them. The Evil Queen clenches her fists. It has been a long time since she has had to fight a creature with her bare hands. She seems to remember a good deal of slapping.

And then there's the sound of Dracula's footsteps leaving, and the door shuts behind him. Moanica exhales. The Evil Queen is only slightly disappointed to have missed an opportunity for a slap fight.

"That was close," says Moanica.

The Evil Queen creeps from her hiding place and unbends the spikes on her shoulder pads. The books she was reading (*Wuthering Frights*, *A Tale of Two Beasties*, and a reference guide titled *The Monster*

Manual of Vile) are no longer on the table. Dracula must have put them back on the shelf. And he left behind an ornate wooden box.

"What is this?" the Evil Queen asks.

"Um, a box?" says Moanica.

The queen examines the box, alert for traps, and then opens it.

"Are you familiar with this?" the Evil Queen asks.

Moanica edges closer, a scroll in her hand. "Oh... yes! That's the Monster Mapalogue. Or at least part of it. There's a necklace bit to it, too."

The Evil Queen taps a fingernail on the wooden map. "This," she says. "Have you seen *this* hexact map before?"

"Well, there's Monster High," she says, pointing with the scroll she's holding, "and over there is the cemetery where I used to live, but I've got no idea what that 'Ever After' thing is. Never seen those other places on a map before. I can't even read them."

The Evil Queen stares at the map. A shame most of the lands aren't labeled. It is much easier to use magic on things if you know their names.

"What do you suppose *Wander*land is?" Moanica asks, pointing at the map again with her scroll. "Maybe people there just wander around confused all the time."

"*Wonder*, not *wander*. But you're mostly right," the Evil Queen says. She notices Moanica's pointing tool. "What is that?"

"Wonderland," Moanica says.

"No, you fool, the scroll," the Evil Queen says. "Where did you get that?"

"From behind the shelf. It must've fallen. I hoped it was a secret book, but it's just old wallpaper."

The Evil Queen plucks the scroll from Moanica's hands and unrolls the edge of a document covered in letters that are, in fact, *not* wallpaper designs. She traces her finger down the lines of characters. "This is another language," she says.

"No way," Moanica says. "I know French, and that is not French."

"Quiet, fiend!" the Evil Queen hisses. "I'm trying to translate it!"

In proper circumstances—that is, if she were in her castle in Ever After, surrounded by magical objects and universally recognized as the magnificent ruler of all she surveyed—the Evil Queen would have been able to magically translate the document and absorb its information. But these are not normal circumstances.

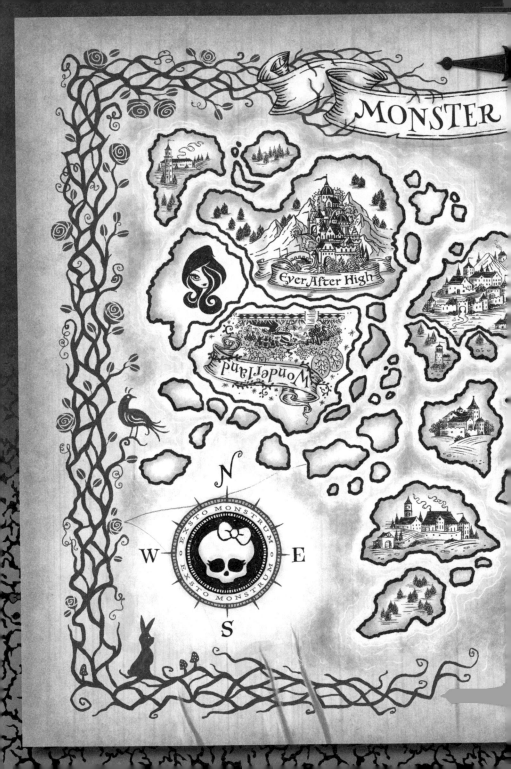

MONSTER

Ever After High

Wonderland

EXSTO MONSTRUM
EXSTO MONSTRUM

N

W   E

S

Her fingers glow with dim light as she casts the translation spell, managing only a character or two before she must cast the spell again. It is like trying to read by flickering candlelight that the wind blows out every few seconds.

"What's the title?" Moanica asks, pacing behind the Evil Queen as she works.

"'*The...Path...of...Shadow,*'" the Evil Queen reads. A way to Shadow High! At last!

"Well, that's a good sign," Moanica says. "Ancient scroll, hidden behind a bookcase, secret knowledge. What else does it say?"

The Evil Queen continues to read. "There is a subtitle. '*The Cautious Vampire's Guide...to...*'"

"To what?"

A muscle beneath the queen's eye begins to twitch.

"'*To Summer Walks on the Riverside...*'" the Evil Queen says through clenched teeth. "Walks on the riverside? Vampires are supposed to be *evil!*"

"Evil? Who, Dracula?" says Moanica. "One time I saw him knit a tea cozy."

"*Gah!*" The Evil Queen throws the scroll down. Magical energy crackles around her fingertips. "I am surrounded by fools!"

A card flutters out of the scroll. Moanica picks it up.

"Well, it looks like Dracula is a *little* evil," she says. "This scroll was checked out from some library and is, like, *literally* a thousand years overdue. That's a serious fine."

"What library?" the Evil Queen asks.

Plop.

"What was that noise?" Moanica asks.

"I don't know," the Evil Queen says. "You said something about a library?"

Plop. Plop.

"What *is* that?" Moanica asks.

The Evil Queen plucks the card from Moanica's hand.

Plopplopplop.

"Can't you hear that?" Moanica asks. "It's driving me crazy!"

"Oh, I can hear it," the Evil Queen says, reading the card. "I'm just ignoring it."

The card in her hand is a checkout slip for the scroll, from a place called the Lost Library, and if the date on the slip is accurate, the library is ancient.

PLOP.

"*Agh!*" Moanica groans. "We either have to find out what that is or get out of here. I hate that sound."

PLOP, PLOP.

"I'm growing to like it, actually," the Evil Queen says. "Because I think it means someone or something is trying to stop me. And when someone tries to stop me, it usually means I'm on the right track."

The plopping sound ceases, and the Evil Queen laughs. She *is* on the right track. She'll continue her library hopping, then. She knows the Lost Library's name. But who is trying to stop her?

Narrators, she thinks.[50] The Wonderland child has already given her a clue. *Narrators. They're real. They're trying to stop me. Which means ... they* fear *me.*

She smiles wickedly, transitioning easily into a truly magnificent evil laugh.

"Ugh," Moanica whispers. "You are really bad at being sneaky!"

---

50 This is not good. This is so not good.

CHAPTER 13

RAVEN IS NOT SOUND ASLEEP. SHE'S ALSO NOT dead asleep, sleeping like a baby, or any of the other ways Narrators describe people who are *deep* asleep (she's not that, either). She *is* sleepy. And also extremely uncomfortable.

While Raven is generally a fan of sleepovers, the before-sleep part is the best—chatting and snacking and playing Ever After games like pin-the-horn-on-the-unicorn or *Rock Bard* on the MirrorStation 5. The sleeping part of sleepovers is less fun, especially tonight, when it requires trying to sleep on Headmaster Grimm's hard office floor.

"The headmaster told us to stay put till he gets back," Apple had said.

"When will that be?" Raven asked.

"Morning, maybe?" said Apple. "He seemed pretty spooked by the tremors and the appearance of the"—she lowered her voice to a whisper—"*the monsters*. We'd better just crash here tonight."

A squeak rouses Raven. She knows by the soft inhale and exhale of their breaths that the other girls are all dead asleep. But Raven is fairy aware of the hard floor under her hip and head, the high ceiling above her, and the blank stares of various creature statues. And somewhere out there is her mother, who, she'd bet every shoe in her closet, is *not* playing patty-cake-bake or *Rock Bard*. When her mother plays games, they are far more dangerous.

"What are you up to, Mom?" Raven whispers into the darkness.

And then—*crash*.

The floor beneath her buckles; the books on the shelves pop off and thump onto the ground. A lifelike troll statue tips and falls face-first right beside Raven.

"*Ow!*" says the troll statue.

"Wait, you're alive?" says Raven.

"No," it says, its plastic lips pressed against the floor. "Never was. Come on, you think Headmaster Grimm went hunting and came back with me? I'm just a decoration, bought from a gift catalog."

"Then how can you talk?" she says.

The troll statue winks. "It was a *fancy* gift catalog."

A second tremor hits, even larger than the first. Raven ducks under a table, her hands over her head, expecting the roof to come down. The stones of the school groan like stomachs full of peas porridge in the pot nine hundred days old.

When the tremor passes, the school is still standing. Raven sends a spark of magic to turn on the lights.

"Everybody okay?" she asks, righting the troll statue.

"Thanks," the statue says.

"You're welcome?" Raven says. She isn't sure what proper etiquette is when dealing with large troll-like figures that are actually just plastic decorations magicked into talking. But it never hurts to be polite.

The girls are all standing, checking themselves over. Frankie is sewing her leg on tighter. Apple is pulling tiny puffs of dust out of her hair.

"Where's Maddie?" asks Raven.

"Oh!" says Apple, looking around. "I don't know. She was asleep right next to me."

"Maybe she wandered off?" says Frankie.

Draculaura smiles. "She does seem the type of person to wander...."

"*Or* to stand on a balcony singing to the moon and get snatched by a mob of shambling Things," says the troll statue.

"What?" says Raven.

"What?" says Apple.

"What?" say Draculaura and Frankie at the same time.

"What?" says the troll statue. "It was just an observation."

"Do you mean," says Apple, looking up at the troll statue with her hands on her hips and her best no-nonsense expression, "that you saw some persons of unknown origin abducting Madeline Hatter from that balcony?"

"I don't *mean* to say anything," explains the troll statue. "But somehow I do, all the same."

"Well, surely we'll find Maddie soon," says Apple. "In the meantime, Ever After High's school rules hexplicitly state that in the event of an earthquake, all students should evacuate the building and meet in a safe location. So we should really get moving!"

Raven, knowing better than to argue, magicks the door unlocked and follows Apple out. Behind her, Draculaura whispers, "School rules. Real high schools have those."

"Yeah," says Frankie. "We should totally come up with some great school rules for Monster High when we get back. I mean, *if*. I mean—"

"*When*," says Draculaura.

"Yeah, when," says Frankie.

But neither sounds certain.

There's a nice full moon outside, filling the courtyard with a trembling blue light and lining all the gathered students in silver. Raven glances at the two monster girls, half expecting one of them to howl at the moon or turn into a furry creature or something.

That's the sort of stuff that happens in campfire tales. But no, they just huddle together, looking around with wide eyes.

"So foggy," says Draculaura.

"Yeah," says Frankie. "I love a foggy night. But something about that fog…"

"It's weird, isn't it?" says Raven looking into the dark fog. "It almost looks…solid."

The full moon lights up a thick wall of fog at the edge of the school grounds. But that's the thing—the fog stays there around the borders of Ever After High, not rolling in, not diminishing.

Raven walks closer. She feels more than a bit squeamish, her belly flipping and flopping like a fish, as if warning her that she's about to see something alarming.

She reaches out her hand and touches the fog, trailing her fingers through it. Just air, a little damp, a little chilly. Like your basic fog. But then Raven looks down, screeches, and stumbles away.

"Everyone, stay back!" she yells at the gathered students. "Where the fog starts, the ground ends. It just ends! We're…like, trapped on an island!"

"What do you mean, *ends?*" asks Apple, hurrying to her.

Raven grabs Apple's hand and pulls her back before she can fall into the fog and down, down, down into the nothing or whatever is down there.

Now everyone is screaming and running around. The fog extends around the grounds, completely circling the school. Most run back inside, as far from the fog as they can get.

Raven takes out her MirrorPhone and tries to call her dad in his castle in a nearby kingdom. Nothing. No signal.

"I can't reach my mom, either," says Apple. "It won't even dial."

"Apple!" says Briar Beauty,[51] running toward her friend. She's wearing pink pajamas and fluffy bunny slippers, and her long brown hair is in braids. Her cheeks, normally several shades darker than Apple's, are flushed pink from worry. "It's not just the MirrorPhones that aren't working. I checked the wishing well, too, and it's...it's *empty*. No water, just

---

51 Daughter of Sleeping Beauty, Apple's BFFA, and one seriously stylish chick.

fog down in its depths. And when I dropped a pebble into it, I never heard it hit bottom. It's like we're trapped."[52]

"Briar, the faculty is gone and Maddie is missing. Can you get everyone back to their rooms and find me if there's any word?"

Briar nods and runs off, her bunny slippers squeaking cheerfully with each step, as if they don't know that Ever After High is having the worst crisis in forever after. Which they probably don't. Since they're just fluffy footwear. But earlier in this chapter, a decorative troll statue spoke, so *you just never know.*

Anyway, Raven speed-dials Maddie's dad, the Mad Hatter. He lives just across the bridge from Ever After High, in the Village of Book End, but even that call won't go through.

"Is Book End gone?" Apple squints in that direction, but the fog is so thick it's impossible to tell.

They run toward the bridge. The wall of fog

---

52 In Ever After, wishing wells are, like, the second-most-common form of transportation, right after walking and right before unicorn-breath-powered hybrid carriages.

crosses over it, but as they get closer, they see that the bridge itself has been sliced clean in half.[53]

"Apple," says Raven, "what if Maddie was trying to go home to her dad when…?"

Apple grabs Raven's hand and squeezes.

"Maddie!" Raven yells into the night, magically projecting her voice louder. "Maddie, if you can hear me, answer please!"

No answer.

"Maddie, this is Apple!" says Apple. "Right now I'm standing on my head and making a pot of noodles with my feet while oinking like a pig!"

No answer.

"Well, that settles it," says Apple. "If she didn't come running to see me stand on my head and make noodles with my feet while oinking, then she's nowhere nearby. But surely she's not down…down there, wherever that fog is coming from."

Raven is whispering under her breath and holding a spark of blue light in her hands. She rolls it like a ball of clay, and with the final words "Go find

---

53 Can you imagine if you woke up and your house was suddenly cut off from the rest of the world? I would completely flip out!

Maddie!" she lets go of the blue light. It zips up into the air, then zaps back and forth, inside the school, under the nose of a dazed-looking ogre, over Daring Charming so fast it leaves his perfectly coiffed hair in a rat's nest, and back to Raven.

The ball of light settles into her hand with a sad little sigh, flattens, and disappears.

"Maddie isn't at Ever After High," says Raven. "Then where is she?"

"Um, I know we're new here," says Draculaura as she and Frankie catch up with Raven, "and I don't know what fancy-catalog troll statues are like in Ever After, but maybe it was right? About the Things taking her?"

"Come with me," says Raven.

"Where?" asks Frankie.

"Here," says Raven, pulling the two girls closer to her and Apple. She mutters some words and grabs their arms, and suddenly, all four are rocketing into the air.

"*Uhhhhhh…*" says Frankie.

"*Aaaaah!*" says Drac.

"*Wahooo!*" cheers Apple. "Raven, you've been practicing this spell! It's so much better than that time you shot us headfirst into the royal horse stables!"

"Horse stables?" says Draculaura. *"AAAAH WAAAH!"*

They rocket straight toward Maddie's dorm room window. Her closed window.

Raven mutters another quick spell, and a second before they crash into the window glass, it turns into strawberry gelatin. They smash through the rubbery dessert, cubes of it flying everywhere, and land on Maddie's bed.

"Sorry about the strawberry gelatin," says Raven. "I couldn't think of anything else that fast." Then she mutters, "Anyway, I always thought crashing through gelatin would be kinda fun."

Apple straightens her tiara, Frankie jolts with a random spark of electricity, and Draculaura collapses on the floor.

"If people were meant to fly"—she gasps—"they would have been born bats."

Raven is checking on Maddie's bed and desk, inside her spare hats and teapots, and under a laundry hamper shaped like a mushroom—all the usual places where Maddie keeps things.

"There's no note!" says Raven. "Maddie didn't leave a note!"

Briar rushes in. "No sign of Maddie. And Lizzie Hearts says Kitty has disappeared, too!"

"But, um, isn't that kind of Kitty's thing?" says Raven. "Disappearing?"

"You're right," says Briar. "I'll keep looking." She runs off again, slippers still squeaking.

"Kitty Cheshire, too!" says Apple.

"Fairytale and Wonderland characters running around..." Frankie sits on a hat-shaped chair, her head in her hands. "I'm never going to get used to this place."

"Um, Frankenstein is your *dad*," Apple whispers.

Raven's head is down, her eyes closed in concentration. Her magic has gotten better with her studies, but Baba Yaga says for a sorceress, casting a spell should be as easy as casting a pebble. And though Raven's magic rarely backfires now and can look easy, sometimes casting a spell still feels like hauling a bag full of pebbles upstairs while wearing ice skates and singing the alphabet backward.

A blue glow drifts off Raven's hands like smoke and then darts to Kitty's bed, which is on one side of her and Maddie's shared room. The glow outlines an invisible human form curled up on the bed. Green eyes fade into the outline, lavender hair pulls loose from a fat braid, and a chin quivers.

"Kitty!" Apple exclaims. "You're here!"

"Here and there, I'm neverwhere," Kitty says.

"What does that even mean?" Draculaura asks.

"Wonderlandians don't always make sense," Apple explains.

"Less sense when dense gents from across the fence make hence with friends," replies Kitty.[54]

"Um," Frankie says, "is that a poem or something?"

Kitty takes a deep breath and says, "They took Maddie."

"*Who* took her?"

"A girl with them…she called them…Zomboyz."

"I don't think that's a word," Apple says.

"Oh, it's a word," Draculaura says. "It's the first thing Kitty has said that makes sense to me."

"The Zomboyz are…well, they're a pack of zombies," says Frankie.

Apple jumps to her feet. *"Zombies are real?"*

Everyone blinks at her. Apple sits back down.

"Sorry. Sorry, I don't think I'll ever get used to this."

---

54 Kitty is speaking Riddlish. It's a Wonderland thing.

"Tell me about it," Frankie mumbles.

"The girl must be Moanica, the leader of the Zomboyz pack," says Draculaura. "Basically, they follow her around and do whatever she says. But why is Moanica in Ever After? And what would she want with Maddie?"

Kitty is still shivering, so Raven takes the blanket from Maddie's bed and puts it over her.

"I saw them carrying her," says Kitty. "Right into the fog. Some of them came after me. They didn't talk, just grunted, but I heard a...a Narrator say that the Zomboyz were looking for Wonderland girls who smell like madness and magic. I went In-Between, so they couldn't grab me."[55] She sniffs, her chin still quivering. "Usually in the In-Between, I can travel anywhere in Ever After, and a lot faster than I can in the real world. But I couldn't get to Book End or anywhere off campus. The fog—it's like there's nothing out there. The rest of Ever After is just...gone! I don't know what's happening, but I'm just going to go curl up in the In-Between till it's all fixed again.

---

[55] The In-Between is the place where Cheshires go when they disappear.

You'll fix it, right, Apple? Raven? You'll find Maddie and you'll fix it?"

Raven's stomach is doing that impressive fishy-like flipping and flopping, but she nods. Kitty looks relieved as she fades away, her frown the last part of her to disappear.

CHAPTER 14

"HOW COULD MOANICA BE HERE?" FRANKIE ASKS. IT doesn't make any sense to her, but then very little of what has happened since she messed up their history project has made sense.

"Who is Moanica?" Apple asks. She grabs Frankie's arm and looks up at her with panicked eyes. "Is she a monster, too? Are monsters behind all this? Did *you* cause the tremors and Maddie's kidnapping and...and that scary fog?"

"What? No!" says Frankie. "I mean, I don't think I did. I mean, no! I mean, I don't think so. But..."

Of course she didn't kidnap Maddie! But...but did she cause the tremors? When she tried to get the

Mapalogue to send them to Shadow High, she didn't know *what* she was doing. Apple's suspicious stare feels like a condemnation.

"But Moanica *is* a monster. She's one of our classmates," Draculaura says. "One of the more… difficult ones."

"Difficult in what way?" Apple asks. "Our classmate Faybelle once cast a wilted-wings spell on the other fairies trying out for a role in the school play to improve her chance of getting the part. It took days to wear off, and the poor fairies were so depressed that they couldn't even cheerhex. Difficult like that?"

"That might be the definition of difficult here, but it's not quite what we meant," Frankie says.

Apple purses her lips. "What I'm asking is if she's the kind of person who would trap perfectly nice, innocent people in some kind of evil fog world."

"I don't think she's capable of creating a pocket universe and hiding fairytale characters in it, no," Frankie says. She knows she's being more snarky than she should, but something about monsters being blamed for everything irritates her.

"Yeah, I don't know what a 'pocket universe' even is," Raven says.

"Me neither," Draculaura says.

"A pocket universe is kind of a quantum bubble of space-time," says Frankie.

"Yes, it's where a parallel reality theoretically can unfold," Apple says.

"Oh thanks, that clears it right up," Draculaura says, and Raven smiles.

Frankie's neck bolts sizzle and a twitch of electricity tingles upward, heating the tips of her ears. That happens when she's angry—specifically, jealous. And she's ashamed to realize that she is a little jealous of how Draculaura seems to have made an insta-connection with this daughter of the Evil Queen, while Frankie is feeling like Alice lost in Wonderland.

"Okay, then," Frankie says with a deep breath, trying to defizzle. "I'm just surprised that Apple here has ever met anyone in fairytale-land who is even the slightest bit difficult."

"Well, surprising as it may seem, I have," Apple replies, trying hard to keep her voice light.

"If you say so," Frankie says.

That sounds mean, and Frankie frowns at herself. Apple frowns in response, as if she thinks Frankie is frowning at her.

"*Okaaay, ghouls…*" Draculaura says, making a "calm down" gesture.

"And frankly, *Frankie*," Apple says, "it seems a little petty to assume I haven't had challenges just because I'm a princess. My mom rules an entire kingdom and often has to deal with difficult situations. It's part of my story."

Frankie's ears are red-hot, and even her eyelashes vibrate with loose electricity.

"Whoa, now," Raven says. "I think all this fog might be clouding our thinking."

"Ha," Draculaura says. "I see what you did there. '*Cloud* our thinking'? Clever."

"I thought it might have been too subtle," Raven says with a smile.

Apple is staring at Draculaura and Raven with the same kind of confused, annoyed, and jealous expression that Frankie fears is on her own face.

"I didn't think it was funny, either," Frankie whispers to Apple.

Apple glances at her and quirks a little smile.

"*Anyway,*" Frankie says, loud enough to interrupt the giggle party just starting between Draculaura and Raven, "I think the answer is that Moanica is difficult in a pretty bad way. She loves to cause chaos. But she couldn't be responsible for this weird fog wall that's cut your school off from the rest of the world. That's serious business."

Raven glances at the mirror in Maddie's room. "Not on her own, anyway," Raven says.

"I still don't get how Moanica, much less the Zomboyz, could have gotten here at all," Draculaura says.

"We got here," Frankie points out.

"And now we're trapped here," Draculaura says, looking out a window at the fog.

Frankie's blood goes as cold as yeti feet. *Trapped.* At least when she was locked up in the laboratory she had her dad with her and the hope of one day leaving. Now she's trapped in some school full of people who are frightened of monsters, and she can't even run away. Outside the window, the world is brightening with morning, but the fog stays put.

"Wait," Frankie says.

"Not a problem," Draculaura says. "I was kind of doing that anyway, since there's *nowhere to go.*"

"What if there is, though?" Frankie asks.

"You saw the road to Book End," Raven says. "Where the fog starts, the bridge just ends."

"But Maddie *was* taken away," Frankie says. "Therefore, she was taken *away*! She left Ever After High. Despite the fog, she left. Therefore—"

"There's got to be a way out!" Draculaura says.

"I see only two possibilities," Apple says. "One: She left through a secret wishing well. Or two: She left via a hidden bridge through the fog."

"Wait, what?" asks Frankie. "Those are your only two possibilities? And one of them is 'a secret wishing well'?"

"It's an Ever After thing," Raven says.

Apple taps her finger on her chin. "Briar said that the wishing wells were fog-bottomed."

"So there's got to be a bridge," says Frankie, heading toward the door. "I'll go look."

"I'll come with you," Apple says. "Headmaster Grimm asked us to take care of you, and besides, the students are already a little on edge. If they see a . . . a . . ."

"Monster?" asks Frankie.

Apple shrugs. "As nice as I'm sure you must be, if they see a *monster* creeping about alone, they could get frightened."

"I wasn't planning on *creeping about*, but I see your point," Frankie says.

"Cool!" Draculaura says. "I'll stay with Raven and we'll work on *magic*!"

Frankie follows Apple out into the halls of Ever After High. No coffin lockers, no dangling cobwebs or slime trails, no mysterious gurgling noises from the vents. Instead, it's all filtered sunlight, live trees growing like pillars through the floors and up the walls, humming mushrooms sprouting between their roots, and butterflies—*Wait, do those butterflies have human faces?*—flitting past her nose. It is, in a word, *magical*. Frankie stares. She's never believed magic was real, but she's kinda loving the thought that she might be wrong.

"Briar gathered the students in the Charmitorium for a 'fog party,'" Apple says. "Ashlynn Ella is helping, so at least the students will be—"

"Who is Ashlynn Ella?"

"Oh, she's..." Apple blushes, a pretty pink on her pale cheeks, and mutters, "Cinderella's daughter."

Frankie shakes her head. Her neck makes its usual creaking sound. "Cinderella's daughter...This can't be real—none of this is real...." Not for the first time, Frankie considers that maybe she is still lying in the Mad Science lab at Monster High after being struck by lightning, and this is all just a dream.

"We'll go out the opposite direction of the Charmitorium so no one has to see you," says Apple.

So no one has to see me, Frankie thinks. *In Ever After, I'm some kind of disgusting Thing.*

Frankie groans at the thought, and Apple jumps.

"*Ooh*, please don't make that noise! It's fairy creepy."

"Sorry," Frankie says. Behind them, she hears the distinct popping noise Draculaura makes when turning into a bat, followed by Raven's applause.

At least they're *getting along*, she thinks. Her ear tips are hot again; her hair rises slightly with static. She's not usually a jealous friend. What's gone wrong with her?

Water break. Or…er…scene change. Time jump. Something like that.[56]

Anyway, sometime later, Frankie is hiding behind

---

56 Look, a girl has to keep hydrated when telling a story.

a garden shed as Apple checks to make sure no one is around. Frankie is all too familiar with hiding and prefers for that part of her life to be over.

"The coast is clear," Apple whispers loudly.

Frankie edges out from the shed and paces along the fog.

"You could whistle," suggests Frankie, "instead of trying to whisper at me."

"Well, whistling is close to singing, and it's hard to be sneaky when I sing, because birds start to follow me—"

"Wait, birds follow you?"

Apple shrugs. "Birds like me. If I whistle, they might think I'm in distress and come to my rescue."

"*Okaaay.* Well, this might go faster if we split up." Frankie sees nothing out there. The land just drops away. It's so creepy it gives her a happy kind of jolt in her heart region.

"What? Are you kidding?" Apple asks. "Never split up! That's when they get you!"

"When who gets you?"

"The monsters!" Apple blurts. "Well…*other* monsters. Evil ones."

"You know, I think you might be underestimating

your fellow students," Frankie says. "This fog is way scarier than I am, and they're currently having a *party* hosted by Sleeping Beauty's daughter in bunny slippers. Maybe we don't need to worry about hiding me so much?"

A branch cracks somewhere behind them.

Apple shoves Frankie to the ground. "Quick, pretend to be a rock."

Frankie moves to get back to her feet, but Apple sits on her.

"*Dum-dee-dum-dee-dum,*" she sings. "Nothing to see here. Just Apple White sitting on a perfectly normal rock."

A rabbit scampers out of a nearby bush, stares at them, and hops away.

"I think it was a rabbit," Apple whispers to her Frankie-chair.

"This isn't working," Frankie mumbles, her face pressed against the grass.

When they return to Raven and Draculaura, they find the room bathed in purple light. A hairbrush is on the table, a thin purple mist surrounding it.

"Okay," Raven says. "Now spin it."

Draculaura hits the handle of the hairbrush and

it spins on the top of the table like a deranged clock. After a few rotations, it suddenly hops off the table, clatters to the floor, and scoots itself under the desk. The glow fades, and Raven sighs.

"Are walking brushes normal here?" Frankie asks.

"You're back!" Draculaura says. "Did you find a bridge?"

"No," Apple says. "No bridge, and also walking brushes are not normal."

"That all depends on your definition of *normal*," Raven says. "But no progress here, either. I'm trying to enchant objects to go find my mom, but nothing works. I think they might be afraid of her."

Under the desk, the brush, a plush bear, and a copy of *Princess Today* magazine all shiver.

Frankie runs her mint-green fingers over Maddie's desk. Not much open space for doing homework; it's taken up by two pairs of tiny running shoes that look small enough to fit a mouse, a basket of bright-purple muffins, several dozen teapots, a collection of shoelaces, a stack of books so high it tilts in the draft but never falls, and various other items Frankie has no name for, though her curious brain aches to figure them out. Maddie seems like the kind of person anyone would want to seek out. Even a hair-brush.

"Would the spell work better if the brush were trying to find Maddie?" Frankie asks.

"Maybe," says Raven. "Or...*ooh*! I know! In order to do a stronger, long-distance seeking spell, I need something that belongs to Maddie."

Of all the various teacups in the room, one appears to be more well used than the others, with tea stains in the bottom and an affectionate chip in the rim.

"How about this?" Frankie asks.

"Hexcellent!" Raven says. "Put the teacup on the table."

With her left hand, Raven makes a gesture, and the teacup begins to spin around and around. With her right hand, she points at the spinning cup and chants.

Glow show the go flow.

A green fog surrounds the cup, forming a perfect sphere.

Raven clenches her teeth and spins her left hand harder. The green sphere forms the barest sugges-tion of a point.

"*Gah!*" Raven exhales. The sphere disappears and the cup comes to a stop.

"Was it working?" Draculaura asks.

"I think so," Raven says, massaging her hand. "But I can't keep that up. It needs to spin at a constant rate so the magic can detect where its spin is different from the natural state of matter."

"Oh, so it's like a gyrocompass," Frankie says.

"What?" the three other girls say at once.

"Ships use compasses to navigate, right?" says Frankie. "But the big ones are full of metal and magnets, which throw off the magnetic field. With a *gyrocompass*, an electric motor spins the compass at a constant speed, and *gravity* naturally pulls a floating needle in the direction of true north. So Raven's left hand is the magical motor, and her right is the magical gravity."

"That sounds about right," Raven says. She holds up her hand. "But my magical motor is cramping."

"Give me a second," Frankie says, glancing around the room.

She takes apart an alarm clock and a makeup case she finds on Kitty's side of the room. Raven fetches some tools, and before long Frankie puts the parts back together to form a spinning mechanism. When she wires the device to the bolts in her neck, the dial begins to spin as fast as a windmill in a storm.

"And you're certain that isn't magic?" Raven asks.

"It's science," Frankie says, handing the device to Raven. "Well, engineering, technically. And plain old electricity makes it go. Put Maddie's teacup in here and the device can keep it spinning for you as long as I'm connected to it."

Frankie attaches the cup to the device with metal clamps, keeping it firmly in place. Raven casts the seeking spell on the cup as Frankie gets the compass spinning again. A misty green sphere surrounds the device, and a small arrow pokes out, pointing to the door.

Draculaura pops into bat form. "Follow that arrow!" she says.

The two princesses and two monsters make their way down the stairs and out toward the wall of fog.[57]

---

57 Oh my bolded text, I have no idea what's going to happen. What is that fog wall? How did the rest of Ever After just suddenly get cut off? Why does my first solo narration have to be such a dangerous story?

CHAPTER 15

RAVEN TAKES THE LEAD, CREEPING THROUGH Lizzie Hearts's Wonderland garden toward a wall of fog as high as the sky. The compass shivers in Raven's hand. Or is she the one who is shivering? Is the land tremoring again?

It could also be Lizzie's hedgehogs, who are rubbing up against Raven's ankles, their shivery backs vibrating with alarm.

"Poor little things," says Raven. "Don't worry. We'll figure out what that nasty fog is and get rid of it, okay?"

The hedgehogs squeak, curl up into balls, and roll away.

The compass arrow points at a place in the wall of fog that looks exactly the same as the rest, certain to lead dead off the sudden cliff.

"Oh curses," says Raven.

"Drac, can you…?" Frankie asks.

Draculaura takes a deep breath and pops back into her bat form with a nervous little squeak. She flaps out into the fog and flies back a moment later.

"A bridge!" she says. "There's a narrow bridge of land, as white as the fog, so it's hard to see, but it's there!"

"A small bridge leading off a mysterious cliff into a foreboding fog," says Raven. "That doesn't sound scary at all. Good thing there aren't monsters involved!"

Draculaura laughs. Frankie and Apple smile nervously at each other. The compass spins, pointing them forward.

Raven sighs and takes the first step through. The wall of fog is so thick she can see nothing, feel nothing but a chill and a damp cold. But then she's past it and in a space of thinner fog. She steps on something solid. A white stone bridge about ten feet wide extends into the distance.

"Is it the *right* way?" Frankie asks. "It's so small

and so well hidden. There might be other bridges out there."

The teacup in the compass is still spinning, but the glow has disappeared.

"Weird," Raven says. "Let me just start this back up again." She smiles as if she's totally confident in her compass-magic abilities. Smiles as if she isn't racked with worry that her mother has already ruined everything, no matter what they do. As if Maddie isn't missing and possibly in terrible danger.

Frankie holds the compass device. Raven casts the locating spell, and . . . nothing.

She tries again. Nothing. No magic. She gets a few green sparks to spit from her fingertips, but that's it.

"What's happening?" Frankie asks.

"I don't know," Raven says. "My magic . . . just isn't working."

Apple makes a face like someone gave her an apple with a worm in it. "Oh dear. Has this happened before?"

"No," Raven says, flapping her hands. "Not like this. Even when I was little, the magic was still there, just . . . smaller. And less manageable."

Flap, flap, flap.

"Um, why are you flapping?" Apple asks.

Raven hops on one foot, and then the other. She waves her arms in the air.

"Something feels different," she says. "Lighter. Do you guys feel that?"

Apple, Frankie, and Draculaura look at one another. "No," they say.

"But we aren't hopping around and flapping our arms," Frankie says. "Maybe that has something to do with it." Frankie leans over to Apple, whispering, "Does she do the flapping to cast spells or something?"

Raven continues to hop. "I feel lighter. It's so strange. Like walking on one of those huge, sproingy plants that bounce you higher when you jump? You know the ones, Apple."

"She's talking about fairy fungus," Apple says. "Kids love it. You can bounce for hours."

"Do you think magic has weight?" Frankie asks. "Because—and I'm not saying I *completely* believe fairytale magic isn't just unexplained science—but if whatever you call magic is real, it might actually weigh something. If it were taken from Raven, she would feel lighter. And that would explain why she can't do her tricks anymore."

"Not *tricks*, Frankie. Magic," Apple says. "Raven, could this place have taken your magic away? Quick, go back to Ever After High!"

Raven hurries back through the wall of fog. Midskip and mid-fog-wall, she comes down hard. A hedgehog squeaks at her landing and chitters angrily as it scurries away.

"*Oof*," Raven says. "Well, I'm off the fairy fungus. Everything's heavier." She gestures, and a little green butterfly springs into existence, flutters around her head, and vanishes. "And the magic is back."

"It's that place that is magic-free, not you," Apple says, Draculaura and Frankie trailing her back through the wall of fog. "That's good news."

"So in the fog, where we most need it, our Maddie compass won't work," Frankie says. "Without your magic, it's just an electric teacup spinner."

"Let me try something," Raven says. She lays a finger on the compass and chants.

Be now a kinder finder,
make your nature true
and fate your school.

Bind power to point
to steel and joint.
Go, become, be one.
The seeds are sown,
so fuel this lark
with spin and arc
alone!

While Raven speaks, a glow surrounds the compass again, but when she ends the spell, the glow sucks into the compass rather than circling the air around it.

"Whew, it worked!" says Raven. "I enchanted the object, so I don't have to keep recasting the spell."

"Simply spelltacular, Raven!" cheers Apple.

Until she did it, Raven hadn't known just how much she needed a win. Just one thing today that maybe she could do right. Suddenly a scary bridge through a world of fog didn't feel impossible.

Maddie would say, *Impossible? I do six impossible things before breakfast, and so can you, Raven Queen!*

Raven's throat feels dry. She says, "We need to find Maddie."

Frankie flips on the compass spinner and crosses back into the fog. Raven takes a deep breath. The spell has left her feeling shaken and half-empty, like an autumn gourd.

"It works!" Frankie calls back. "It isn't quite as glowy as before, but it's pointing us to this bridge."

"Over the river and through the fog, to Madeline Hatter we go!" And Raven starts down the narrow bridge through a mysterious foggy landscape, accompanied by monsters.

The good, hopeful feeling stays with Raven for some time. She imagines it's like Cerise's warm red hood and cloak, protecting her as she walks through a forest of fog. Just as it occurs to her that most forests have big bad wolves in them, she spies movement in the fog ahead.

Raven peers. A darting shape, gray, shaggy, long snout and tail. Is that…is that a wolf? Perhaps a big bad one? Way too coincidental that she thinks about a wolf and one suddenly appears. Her imagination must be playing tricks on her.

The shape darts over the bridge. Raven shuffles

close to the edge and squints into the mist. Nothing. Then she looks straight down. Not nothing.

"Whoa," Raven says, stepping backward. "There's lava down there. Like, bubbling volcanic lava!"

Apple and Frankie peer over.

"I saw it when I was flying over," Draculaura says, staying right where she is. "But I didn't want to talk about it, because, you know, *scary.*"

"Maybe let's go single file from now on," Frankie suggests.

Raven agrees, and the girls continue on.

"I wonder if my mother's magic isn't working out here, either," Raven says.

"Probably," Frankie responds, "if she's anything like you."

Raven stiffens.

"*Ix-nay on the om-may,*" Apple whispers.

"Was that a spell?" Draculaura asks. "I thought only Raven could do spells!"

"It was pig latin," Frankie says.

"*Pig* latin?" Draculaura says. "I have *so many* questions!"

"She was saying not to mention my mom," Raven says. "But don't worry about it."

"Oh, I totes get it," Draculaura says. "Like, if the Normies back home knew my dad existed, they'd assume he was evil, but he's the sweetest guy ever."

"Yeah," Raven says, "hexcept my mom really is evil. If not for her, we wouldn't even be here. You guys would be safe in your school. Maddie would be home. Everything would be fine."

"But I would never have met you, Raven," Draculaura says. "And that would be a shame."

"Thanks, Drac. I just wish it had been under less...apocalyptic circumstances."

Ahead, the bridge forks in two directions. Frankie checks the compass and leads them to the left.

"Okay...I'm trying to work this out," Frankie says. "Even though she's technically evil, does your mom still love you?"

Does she? Raven certainly hoped so when she was little. And now? She's not sure anymore. She doesn't care, she tells herself, but her heart makes a twisting sensation. Raven tries to conjure a true image of her mother in her mind, analyze it for signs of real, genuine maternal affection. But before she can find a way to sum up her relationship with her mother, a dark figure saunters down the bridge toward them.

Not exactly the Big Bad Wolf, but all the same Raven wishes for Cerise's red cloak.

"What in Ever After is that?" asks Apple.

"Nothing in Ever After," says Raven. "We're not in Ever After anymore."

"You all sound like chubby, little chitterbirds," the Evil Queen snaps, her figure resolving out of the mist. "My, I used to love a good roast bird with mustard and pickles!"

Apple makes a noise in her throat like a frog that has swallowed its own tongue. Raven can barely breathe.

"Mother?" Raven says. "What are you—?"

The Evil Queen barrels over her question. "*What* are you wearing, daughter? You don't have a spike on you anywhere! For the sake of my eyeballs, invest in some decent shoulder pads!"

"But—" Raven begins.

"Anyway, my little green friend, of course I love my daughter. In my own, evil way. Isn't that what you would say, Raven?" The Evil Queen is nearly upon them, but she seems to be growing taller. She's like a frightening, sparkly giantess. "And another thing… Wait, who are you again?"

"I...I'm your daughter, Raven," she says in a quiet voice.

"Hmm"—the Evil Queen examines her nails—"your name no longer pleases me. You should change it to Beatriz von Witchiest. Or maybe Imma Gunna Rule. Where are my goblin servants? Come hither, minions, and carve a sculpture of your queen out of ice! No, wait...out of watermelons! No, make it cream cake!"

"Is she usually this chatty?" Frankie asks Apple.

"I...I guess," Apple says. "But when I imagine her, she's a lot more—"

A crash of deafening thunder sounds, and from the fog-stained sky the Evil Queen descends...a *second* Evil Queen. Only this one is glowing and is the size of a small house.

"What the what?" Draculaura yells. "How many Raven's evil moms are there?"

The queen on the bridge does nothing to indicate she has noticed her giant flying twin and continues to talk, commanding absent minions to build her a throne made of ripe peaches and ordering Raven to change her name to things like Missy McEvilton and HeaddressFan217.

The sky Evil Queen raises her hands, a giant ball of fire forming between them. She screams as she hurls the fire straight at Apple.

"No!" Raven shouts, diving to push her friend out of the way. They fall onto the bridge, fire singeing the air inches above them.

"*Oww*..." Apple groans, rubbing her head.

"Hey," Draculaura says. "Giant flying Evil Queen disappeared. Right when Apple hit her head."

The skies are empty of everything but fog. The talking Evil Queen is still on the bridge, though, and still talking.

"How about Spiky Shoulders 'R' Us? No, that would be a hexcellent gift shop but not a great name for a daughter. *Hmm*... Doomlet Von Greatness the Third? Empress Sparklepants?"

"You know, I was kind of scared of her at first," Draculaura says. "But after the big, glowing fireball version, this one is not so scary."

"She appeared after I started thinking about her," Raven says.

"Yeah, me too." Apple rubs her head. "I was thinking how your mom seemed way scarier to me."

Raven nods. "And then a way scarier one appeared."

She closes her eyes. She imagines the last time she saw her mother eating. Dumplings. She was eating dumplings. She loved those things.

"Whoa!" Draculaura says. "Magic food!"

Raven opens her eyes. The chatty Evil Queen is still there. Still ranting. Only now she has a little plate of dumplings.

"Above all, choose a frightening name," the woman instructs. She holds up a finger, plucks a dumpling from the plate, and pops it into her mouth, chewing as she speaks. "Fear . . . is the only . . . universal . . . currency."

"She's imaginary," Raven says. "Something about this place . . . it's making our thoughts real."

"Seriously?" Draculaura squeals. "Hold on a sec."

Raven closes her eyes and mutters, "No mother, not real; no mother, not real," but the woman does not disappear.

The bridge shakes, and suddenly there is a giant frog, much too large to fit on the bridge, crouched behind her imaginary mother.

"*Ribbit*," it thunders.

The talking queen's expression of horrified shock makes Raven smile, and finally the queen vanishes.

"Thanks for that, Drac," Raven says. "I couldn't get her to disappear."

Draculaura smiles. "It helps if you tell a story, I think," she says. "I just started going through a story Dad used to tell me about a giant frog in the swamps that would eat unsuspecting—"

"That's good," Raven says. "Stop there."

"Okay," Draculaura agrees, still smiling.

"*Ribbit*," the giant frog croaks.

"You realize, of course," Apple says, "there is now a giant frog on our path. How do you propose getting rid of it?"

"Apple could kiss it," Frankie says. "Maybe it will turn into a giant prince."

"Haha," Apple says. "*Not* my story."

The frog begins to turn transparent, so that the girls can see the path beyond.

"Is it disappearing?" Raven asks.

"Not really," Drac says. "I just imagined more of the story where the frog turns into a ghost and guards the swamp against evil."

"But it's still *on* the path," Apple says.

Draculaura shrugs. "We'll have to walk through it," she says. "It's a ghost. You can walk through ghosts. I mean, it's *rude* to walk through ghosts, but it was imaginary to begin with, so I don't think it'll mind."

Apple takes a deep breath. "Fine. About to walk through an imaginary ghost frog. Nothing scary here. No problem whatsoever."

One by one, the girls walk through the ghost frog, and it *ribbits* at them each time.[58]

---

58 Okay, I figured out that this weird foggy place must be the Margins. I learned about it in Focal Studies class. The Margins is the space *between* stories. Imagination is powerful here, so the girls should be careful about what they imagine.

CHAPTER 16

THE GIRLS MARCH ON THROUGH THE DISMAL, unchanging scenery. Whatever light illuminates this place doesn't shift—no lowering of sunlight, no shadows, just a constant dim glow from somewhere beyond the fog. It gives the place an eerie feeling, as if they are pacing under a dome, some enormous cage built to hold them. Frankie shivers, feeling well and truly caged.

"We should have gotten *somewhere* by now," Frankie says. "Each of my steps is about half a meter long, and I have taken four thousand six hundred and eight. Nine. Ten."

"You've been counting your steps?" Raven asks. "This whole time?"

"Well, we had to calculate distance somehow." Also, the counting helps Frankie focus her thoughts and not imagine anything scary that might materialize in the fog. "How are you guys keeping track? Magic or something?"

"Um," Raven says, "I'm not keeping track."

Draculaura points into the fog. "Whoa, do you see that?"

"Yes," Apple says, a touch of a groan in her voice. "It's fog. More fog."

"No, up ahead. I think there's an island or something."

The thin bridge of land opens into a wide, round patch of land.

Apple yawns, covering her mouth with a dainty hand. "Hey, Frankie, what time is it?"

Frankie instinctively pulls out her iCoffin, but the clock had stopped when they entered the Margins. "I don't know. Why would you ask me?"

"I figured since you were counting steps, you might be counting seconds, too," Apple says.

"That's just crazy," Frankie says. "Who would count seconds?"

"The kind of person who counts steps?" Apple replies stiffly, as if doing her best to keep the annoyance out of her voice.

"Well, actually," Frankie says, not keeping the annoyance out of her voice, "I can probably figure that out. If each step takes about two seconds, and two times four thousand seven hundred and fifty..."

"Is she really going to do this?" Raven whispers to Draculaura.

"Totes," Draculaura says with a smile.

"That's one hundred and fifty-eight minutes," Frankie says. "Let's round up to one sixty for all the talking.... So it's been just over two and a half hours. What time was it when we left?"

"Let's just say it's bedtime," Draculaura says. "I think we're all tired, and this is a good place to camp."

"I should have brought camping stuff," Raven says.

"I brought provisions!" says Apple, handing out princess pea–butter sandwiches and fairyberry juice boxes.

After they eat, Apple detaches the outer layer of her skirt in a flourish, leaving her to look exactly as she did before, except with a slightly less poofy skirt.

"We can use this to sleep on," she says. "It should be softer than the stone."

She lays out the frilly red-and-gold cloth, but it's not big enough for four of them.

"I sleep on a metal slab at home," Frankie says. "Stone will be just fine for me."

"I'm good with stone, too," Draculaura says.

Frankie knows that Drac's sleeping coffin at home has plenty of cushions, but she also knows that her friend can sleep soundly while hanging upside down in a noisy bat cave, so Frankie supposes she'll be fine.

The girls curl up on the skirt-blanket or stone ground and are soon asleep. Except for Frankie. It is true that she sleeps on a metal slab, but it is *her* slab, and it is comfortably familiar. This stone is not. But she isn't planning to sleep. Someone needs to keep watch. After all, people dream when they are asleep, and sometimes dreams are nightmares, and in a place where thoughts can become solid things...

Frankie is congratulating herself for being such

a good wide-awake guard, when her head nods forward. She gasps and sits upright. She's no longer sitting on the stone ground: four gray walls, shelves of books, tables of gadgets, metal slab beneath her. It *looks* like the lab where she spent her early life, but it appears smaller now, more cramped. Frankie leaps off the slab and paces the perimeter. No windows and no door. This is her dream made real.

"No!" Draculaura screams somewhere outside the lab. "Don't! I'm sorry! I'm sorry!"

"Drac?" Frankie shouts back. She pounds on the walls.

"Don't leave!" Draculaura pleads, sounding even more desperate.

Frankie takes a deep breath. "This isn't real," she whispers to herself. "This wall could be anything. It could be…glass."

The stone wall of the lab grows transparent, revealing Draculaura shouting at four figures that resemble Frankie and their other ghoulfriends Clawdeen, Lagoona, and Cleo. They shake their heads in disappointment and walk away. Draculaura starts to follow them, toward the edge of the island and the fall into lava.

Frankie pounds on the glass. "Drac! It's not real! It's not real!"

Draculaura takes another step.

Frankie stares at her own hand. "This is not a normal hand," she whispers. "This hand is made of solid steel." The hand transforms, and she pounds the glass. It shatters, and then the entire glass wall vanishes and her hand goes back to normal.

Draculaura turns. "Frankie?" she says, and then looks back to the imaginary Frankie and friends in the distant fog. "*Ohhh* . . . right."

"You scared me," Frankie says, pulling her friend into a tight hug.

"Where are Raven and Apple?" Draculaura asks.

Two buildings that most definitely weren't there when they went to bed now squat on the stone: a humble cottage with smoke curling out of a chimney and a dark tower with flashes of purple light sparking from a window.

"Um . . . I'm guessing in there?" Frankie says.

"Let's check the cottage first," Draculaura says. "There might be fairytale porridge."

"Imaginary porridge," Frankie says.

"I'll just imagine it fills me up. What is porridge, anyway?"

"I think it's like soup. Or pudding. Or oatmeal," says Frankie.

Draculaura whispers, "I'm hoping for the pudding option."

Frankie opens the door. Inside the one-room cottage, Apple is sitting by the fireplace, her face red from crying. A woman who looks a lot like Apple except with jet-black hair towers over seven tiny beds.

"You know I love you, dear," says the woman, "but this is a royal disappointment. To me, to your father. Frankly, I think all of Ever After is disappointed in you."

"I'm sorry," Apple whispers.

"I thought I raised you better," the woman says. "But look—you burned the apple cobbler! How can you ever be Snow White if you burn the cobbler?"

"She does exist!" whispers Draculaura, gaping at the apparition of Snow White.

"No, she doesn't!" hisses Frankie. "I mean, not right here, at least! This isn't real."

Apple notices the girls. "What's going on?" she asks.

The false Snow White ignores them all entirely. "Not only did you burn the apple cobbler, but you also forgot to turn in your thronework! And your shoes are scuffed! And you smell like canned beans. You have for years. I just didn't have it in my heart to tell you."

"That isn't your mom, Apple," Frankie says, rushing to her side. "That's...just a...um...It's this weird place we're in! It's making what you dream and worry about actually happen!"

Apple narrows her eyes at the shape resembling her mother. "What a relief! I've *never* burned apple cobbler!"

She swats her hair out of her face, walks over to the now-scowling apparition, and gives it a kiss on the cheek. Snow White and the cottage vanish.

"Whew," Apple says. "That was intense. Thank you. Where's Raven?"

"Well, there's..." Draculaura points.

"I'm going to go out on a limb," says Apple, "and guess that Raven is in that scary, dark tower."

The three girls each take a deep breath and then start to climb the tower's stairs.

CHAPTER 17

ANOTHER FIREBALL LEAPS FROM HER MOTHER'S hands and crashes against the stone ground. Raven rolls out of the way. This isn't her mother. She knew from the moment she woke up to the woman gently brushing the hair from her face and sweetly asking Raven how her nap had been. Her real mother had never done that.

But Raven didn't run away when she should have, because some tiny part of her wished this mother were her real mother.

Then the imaginary mother sprouted giant bat wings and claws, which, generally speaking, was an alarming development. By the time the imaginary mother took to the air with Raven in her claws and then locked the girl in a high tower, Raven was positively done with wishing.

Rapunzel's tower had singing birds and visiting princes. Raven's involved dodging fireballs. Raven is pretty good at dodging fireballs, but there's only so much dodge-space in the topmost room of a high tower.

"If you will not join my side," the fake Evil Queen yells, *"I'll burn the socks off your feet! You'll never wear socks again! You. Will. Be.* Sockless!"[59]

A bolt of electricity zaps from the woman's hand and narrowly misses Raven. And her socks. The energy strikes just above the room's only door.

"Weak and clichéd one-liner, Fake Mother," says Raven. "My real mother would have said something like 'Lightning does ghastly things to your hair and skin, darling, so come stand by me, where your chances of being burnt to a crisp are much lower.'"

The apparition that looks like her mother cackles. "Oh my. Lightning can do such ghastly things to your hair and skin, dear."

---

59 Um, probably not something the real Evil Queen would say, but still pretty upsetting, don't you think?

Okay, Raven thinks. *I'm imagining her. So I have some control over what she says. And does.*

"Andsocanfire!" the queen-thing blurts, casting another fireball.

It's not real. It's not real. It's not real, Raven repeats in her mind as the fireball zooms past her face, missing her by an inch. She smells burnt hair.

"That felt fairy, fairy real," she says.

"Raven!"

Apple, Frankie, and Draculaura rush in through the door.

"It isn't real," Frankie says. "That isn't your mom!"

Another fireball crashes toward them, and Raven shoves them out of its path.

"I know!" Raven shouts. "She still won't go away!"

The false queen raises her right hand, and lightning arcs toward them.

"Watch out!" says Raven, but Frankie lurches in front of the others, taking the full blast. The electricity collects around her, siphoning into her body through the bolts in her neck.

"That *felt* real," she says, smoke curling out of her ears.

"*Wow*, Frankie," Raven says. "You are amazing."

"Maybe this *is* your real mom," Draculaura says.

"It isn't," Raven says. "I just can't seem to…" She shuts her eyes to focus, and when she opens them, the wings have disappeared, but the evil figure still hovers, fire building in her left hand again.

"I can't do my electricity trick with fire," Frankie warns.

"I'm trying to think of a version of her that isn't dangerous, but nothing works!" Raven says.

A fireball streaks toward them, and Raven pulls them down to a crouch. The top of her head is hot; the air sizzles.

"Have you tried not thinking of her at all?" Draculaura asks.

"Believe me, I've tried that for years," Raven says.

And then a squad of bunnies riding on goat-back charges into the room.

"Um…" Frankie says.

Also, the bunnies raise kazoos to their mouths and blow them noisily at the queen.

"Er…" Draculaura says.

The bunnies on goat-back vanish in a puff of pink confetti. The false queen stares with an expression of confusion.

"What the... what was that?" Frankie asks.

Apple raises her hand sheepishly. "That was me. I was just wondering what Maddie would do in this situation, and that's what happened."

"That... is a hexcellent idea," Raven says.

Raven asks herself the same question. And as she imagines the answer, it happens. The menacing metal tables and chairs in the room grow feathers and beaks. They march in formation and squawk at the floating apparition. The fake queen casts fireballs at the bird-furniture, melting them into slag just as a bright cloud forms above her head. The cloud emits a tinny tune like that from a music box, and then it rains multicolored bees. The bees giggle as they fall; then they plink against the queen and disappear with puffs of smoke.

About the time the girls start laughing, the fake Evil Queen finally disappears. Everything inside the tower disappears, except a giant, smiling sweet potato pie.

"Is eating the pie an option?" asks Apple.

The pie gasps in a kind of pastry terror and then vanishes.

The walls of the tower begin to flicker.

"We should probably—" Raven begins to suggest.

The four girls run down the stairs of the tower and almost reach the bottom just as the whole thing vanishes. They thud the rest of the way down.

"Ow," says Apple.

"No more sleeping for today," Frankie says, checking herself over and seeming pleased that she's all in one piece. "Let's keep going."

After firing up the compass to get their bearings, they are off and running. Or walking, actually. They are off and walking.[60]

Another fork in the path and five hundred and eighty-two steps (according to Frankie) later, a dark shape looms over them in the fog. To Raven, it looks like a small mountain with two bent trees growing from its top.

"Is anyone else imagining that's a giant girl-eating sheep?" Apple asks.

To Apple, it apparently looks like a giant sheep.

"A giant girl?" Frankie asks. "Eating sheep?"

"No," Apple says. "A giant sheep. That eats girls."

---

60 Not my best paragraph, but I think I'm generally getting better at this!

"It's neither of those things," Draculaura says. "It's a building."

A building in ruins, to be exact. Towers jut out here and there, some collapsed, some intact, like a grand ancient museum that has weathered earthquakes and a thousand years of neglect. It was built on a white stone island far lower than the bridge on which they're walking, so the structure appears half-buried, a kind of stone weed sprouting from the fog. The girls' path arcs slowly downward until the bridge ends on the stone island dotted with gray boulders. The fog rolls back until it surrounds the island like a wall, just as it did at Ever After High.

Carved on an archway entrance to the building is

ἔχασε τη βιβλιοθήκη

"I don't speak that, whatever it is," says Draculaura.

"Hold on," Raven says. As she emerges fully from the fog, that familiar heaviness settles on her. Her magic is back. She casts a translation spell.

"I'm betting it says *Abandon all hope, ye who enter here*," Frankie says.

"Or maybe *Speak, friend, and enter*," guesses Apple.

"It could be there's something pleasant and wonderful waiting for us inside."

"Really?" Frankie asks.

"I'm trying to use the power of positive thinking," Apple replies.

Frankie cracks a smile.

Purple energy flows from Raven's hands to the letters above the entryway. The magic brightens, creating a circle like a lens, and, looking through it, she sees the letters change.

"Not totally clear," Raven says, "but I think it says *Lost Library*, maybe?"

The magic glow fades, and the letters above the building are replaced with LOST LIBRARY, MAYBE?

"Wow, you weren't kidding about the *maybe*, were you?" Draculaura says.

Raven opens her mouth to explain but is interrupted by the boulders in the courtyard, which have begun to groan. And move.

"Zomboyz!" Draculaura shouts.

Every single "boulder" is standing up, clearly not made of rock at all. They've been shielded by a top-level cloaking spell.

"Mother," Raven breathes.

"Come on, Frankie," says Drac. "We've taken care of the Zomboyz before."

She pops into bat form and emits a sonic scream at one group. Frankie faces another. She rubs her hands together and extends them, and a zigzag spark shoots out. The Zomboyz glow briefly, then continue to shamble forward.

"Um, that worked pretty well last time," says Frankie. "Maybe I'm too drained of electricity?"

"Or my mom enchanted them, shielded them from our attacks!" says Raven.

Draculaura tugs on Raven's arm, pulling her back to the bridge. "There are too many of them. Come on!"

The girls stumble back, and the Zomboyz lurch toward them.

"If only we had all our friends to help," says Frankie. "We're better together."

"A posse of monsters would be fairy helpful right now," Apple agrees. "Raven, throw a fireball!"

"What?" Frankie sputters. "We can't do that! Zombies are people, too, you know!"

The Zomboyz gather at the front of the bridge. The path is narrow here, so in single file they march onward. The girls step back, trying to keep their distance.

"Sorry," Apple says. "I…I've never known any zombies before. This still doesn't feel real to me."

Raven casts a magical barrier between the girls and the approaching horde, but the barrier flickers and fades almost immediately.

"Curses!" she says. "My magic is useless again."

"They've pushed us back into the fog," Frankie says.

Kazoos blare a fanfare, like the announcement of oncoming cavalry. Down the bridge charge a dozen goats, each with a bunny on its back. The goat-bunnies leap over the gathered girls, charging the Zomboyz with a chorus of kazoo honks. The Zomboyz stumble away, confused, their wide eyes even wider.

"*Uhhhhh.*" They moan.

"Hooray!" Frankie cheers, clapping for the riders.

The bunnies press their attack, honking furiously until they push the Zomboyz into the courtyard of the library. Once out of the fog, the goats and bunnies vanish.

"Was that you?" Frankie asks Apple.

"It worked before," Apple says, shrugging.

"Voltageous," Frankie says. "I love the goat-bunnies."

A Zomboy groans louder and tromps back onto the bridge.

Raven's magic is muffled in the fog, but her imagination isn't. She closes her eyes and imagines her pet dragon, Nevermore, who lives with her at Ever After High. Is she lost in the fog? Raven's chest feels tight.

A roar she knows well blasts from above. An enormous purple dragon dives at the Zomboyz on the bridge. They scatter, hurrying back to the safety of the courtyard. Nevermore circles the girls twice and then shrinks to roughly cat size, landing next to Raven.

"What is that?" Draculaura beams at the little dragon.

"My pet. She's a young dragon, but she can biggify herself." Raven's shoulders droop. "But, you know, this isn't . . . this isn't the real Nevermore."

"Imaginary?" Draculaura asks.

"The real one is back there," Raven says, nodding in the direction they came from. "At least, I hope she is."

The dragon, without even changing size, charges a Zomboy approaching the bridge again, and he backs up. She exposes her dragon teeth and hisses.

"Still," Draculaura says, admiring the dragon as she flaps back to Raven. "So cool."

"I guess we can keep them at bay with dragons and goats," Frankie says.

"And bunnies," Apple adds. "With kazoos."

"And bunnies with kazoos," Frankie agrees, smiling.

"But we can't stay here!" Raven says. "The compass is pointing at the Lost Library, so Maddie must be there. And maybe my mom, too. We have to get in."

Frankie taps her fingernail on one of her neck bolts. "You know what? I think I have an idea."

CHAPTER 18

THE EVIL QUEEN THROWS OPEN THE IRON DOOR to the dungeon. The Lost Library was sadly lacking a proper dungeon, so she'd formed one from broken pieces of stone, using willpower and magic. Everything she has done, every spelltacular deed, every takeover and power-grab, she accomplished with willpower and magic. It was a relief to return to full magical power on the island of the Lost Library, but she never lost her willpower.

"And I *will* have more *power*," she says aloud, smiling at her own cleverness.

The single occupant of the dungeon, Madeline Hatter, waves. The Evil Queen's shoulders twitch, and she straightens her cloak. She is uncomfortable with friendly greetings in general.

"You will put that flapping hand away," the Evil Queen proclaims, "and you will tell me the truth!"

"Yes! I will!" Madeline Hatter proclaims right back, stuffing her hand into her pocket.

"You will tell me what they are," the queen says, "where they are, and what their plans are!"

"Yes!" Maddie repeats. "I will!"

"Then speak, Hatling!"

"I shall speak!"

"Yes!"

"About what they are! Where they are! And what their plans are!"

"Get on with it!"

"They! Are! *Hedgehogs!* They are in Lizzie's *garden*! And they plan to *eat*! *To eat...tomatoes!*"

"Hedgehogs? No, you addle-brained tea-swiller! The *Narrators*!"

"*Ooooooh.* The Narrators! I was confused. When you said I would tell *you* what *they* are, I didn't know you meant that *you* would tell *me* what they are. It might have been all the shouting. I mean, I'm used to shouting. Lizzie shouts a lot, too, and…why were we shouting, again?"

The queen conjures a spray bottle from thin air and squirts a single burst of water in Maddie's face.

"Focus, little wretch! *Focus!*"

"*Plegh,*" Maddie spits, shaking droplets of water off her face. "Water? What kind of a person puts plain water in a spray bottle? Let me at least put a tea bag in there."

Back in the height of her glory, the Evil Queen had any number of pet cats in her magnificent castle, as any decent sorceress should. She'd found a spray of harmless water to be a highly effective method of training her kitties not to jump up on her potion table. If it worked on cats, why not Wonderlandians?

"I'll do it again," the Evil Queen says, dangling the bottle menacingly. "You know I will. Tell me what you know."

"Okay, okay," says Maddie. "What I know. I will start with dormice. A single one is called a dormouse—"

"*About the Narrators, you fool!*" the Evil Queen shouts, using the spray bottle again.

Water squirts in Maddie's face, interrupting what was bound to be an excellent exposition on dormice.

"Why, thank you, Brooke," Maddie says, dabbing water off her nose. "Dormice *are* a passion of mine."

"*Aha!*" the Evil Queen bellows. "You speak to them even now!"

"No, no, no," Maddie says. "I was talking to Brooke, not the hedgehogs. There's no way those little guys could hear me from here. I mean, they have good ears, but we all have our limits, you know?"

The queen leans so close their ears almost touch, and she tilts her head to listen.

"When you do that with your head," Maddie whispers into the silence, "you look like a bird."

The queen sprays Maddie in the face again.

"You know," Maddie says, "it looks like you're having fun with that. Can I try spraying you now?"

"Who is Brooke, Madeline?" the Evil Queen asks. "You thanked her earlier."

"Oh, she's this super-nice Narrator girl," Maddie says, not realizing that giving the Evil Queen any information at all about Brooke or any other Narrator might be *extremely dangerous.*

"Oops," Maddie says. "Forget that Narrator stuff I said. Brooke is . . . a river. That babbles. Like me."

The Evil Queen smiles a slow smile. "Names are important, and knowing *Brooke* just may make a spell possible."

"I've never had a spellpossible before," Maddie says. "Is it breakfast food or luncheon food or snack—?"

"They *will* fall," the Evil Queen says, "these Narrators who play dice with our lives, who watch and wheedle, gloating from their hidden towers. I will take the power of the thing they fear, and I will crush them beneath its heel!"

Maddie holds up a finger. "Are you talking to me? Because I didn't catch much of that. Or . . . oh! Are you auditioning for a play? That was a pretty good monologue. Now, are you going to sing sixteen bars of a show tune?"

"I am talking to *them*," the Evil Queen says. "The Narrators. They should know their end is coming. They should fear."

"Fear the . . . heel, right? I got that. You think the Narrators are afraid of boots or something."

"They are afraid of *Shadow High*, little Wonderling,"

the Evil Queen says. "And I am about to become its new headmistress."

The queen chuckles to herself as she exits the dungeon. She picks her way through the crumbling library, stepping over fallen stones, sweeping her velvet cape past wobbly bookcases. One wall has fallen away completely, and she has a view into the vast white haze of the Margins. There are books everywhere, scattered on the floor, open on stone tables, some still resting on ancient shelves. She stands behind a halved pillar of stone, almost as if it were a lectern and she were about to give a speech to the fog beyond. She pulls from her robe the Monster Mapalogue and lays it on the pillar. The map has changed again.

"The Lost Library is here. And look there, *Shadow High* is just where those ancient texts said it would be. Nothing remains hidden from the Evil Queen! Nothing!"

The Evil Queen starts to laugh. She laughs louder and louder, her voice crackling. She's so amused she squirts herself in the face with the spray bottle.

She sputters on water. "Ugh, that really *is* annoying," she says, throwing down the bottle.

Then the Evil Queen gets back to laughing. She raises her hands dramatically, gold fire crackling all around them.

"Narrators," she says, "if you're going to run away, now would be a good time."[61]

---

61 Oh stet, I do *not* like the sound of this!

CHAPTER 19

THE GIRLS ARE STUCK ON THE BRIDGE, ZOMBOYZ advancing into the fog. Any mistake and the girls will tumble over the side, down, down into the lava below. And Frankie's plan is...well, it's not foolproof.

"I'm having second thoughts," says Frankie. "Maybe we should run."

"Run where?" asks Drac.

"Back. Away. I don't know. Lately, my plans cause more trouble than good—"

Ploop. Ploop.

"There's that plopping sound again!" says Frankie.

"More like a long plop," says Draculaura. "A ploop."

Plop-plop ploop. Plop-plop-plop. Ploop.

"You hear it, too?" says Apple. "I swear, it follows us around."

"Wait…" Frankie holds up a green finger. "It's not just random plops now. Long ploops, short plops…It's Morse code. The plops are sending a message!"

Frankie closes her eyes and listens so hard her ears spark. She translates the short and long sounds into letters.*"M-U-S-T-S-T-O-P-Q-U-E-E-N-H-U-R-R-Y-M-U-S-T-S-T-O-P—"*

"'Must stop queen, hurry,'" Apple repeats. "Something is warning us about the Evil Queen!"

Yep, it seems *someone* is using plops to send a message to the characters in a suspicious way! And that is very much against Narrator Rules![62]

Hurry, Raven. Hurry, Apple, Drac, and Frankie. Hurry and get past the Zomboyz so you can stop the Evil Queen!

"Okay, if we can get off the bridge," Frankie says, "your magic should work on the island, right, Raven?"

---

62 But…maybe Mom and Dad are interfering because the Evil Queen is up to something bad. *Paragraphically* bad. Story-ending bad?

Frankie still can't help cringing when she says *magic*. Maybe here magic is more than just unexplained science? She likes knowing the *why* of things, but the only way they are going to get past the Zomboyz right now is with something she doesn't understand. With magic.

"Yeah," Raven agrees. "But before you say it, I can't just make a magic cage to put them in and leave. It will disappear as soon as I go after my mom."

"I thought about that," Frankie says. "What we need to do is trade places with the Zomboyz."

"I don't want to be a zombie, thank you," Apple objects.

"I get what you mean," Drac says. "You want *them* on the bridge and *us* in the courtyard."

"Right," Frankie says. "If we can get them far enough down the bridge, Apple and I can just camp out on the edge of the fog and use our imaginations to block them while you deal with your mom."

"What's to stop them from imagining back at us?" Apple asks. "I don't want to see in real life whatever a Zomboy is imagining."

"I don't think we need to worry about that," Frankie says.

The Zomboy at the front of the advancing pack has stopped and is staring at his foot. He groans, as if only just noticing that he is missing a shoe.

The Zomboy behind him bumps into him, and the one behind him bumps into that one, and so on. Soon, they are all groaning in irritation.

"*Uhhh?*" A Zomboy groans from the back.

"*UHHH!*" The Zomboy in the front groans back. He grabs his ankle, attempting to lift his bare foot up to show the group, but he falls down.

"They aren't the brightest torches in the dungeon," Draculaura says. "As long as Moanica isn't with them, you shouldn't have anything to worry about."

"Okay," Raven says, "but how are we going to get all of them onto the other side of the bridge from us without anyone accidentally falling into the, you know, dangerous depths below?"

Apple raises a finger. "I'd like to go on the record as preferring not to get knocked into the lava."

Frankie pulls out the compass and flips it on.

The glow forms, pointing in the direction of the library. "We're in the fog," Frankie says. She holds up the compass. "This is magic. Why is it still working?"

"It's enchanted," Raven says. "We did it back at Ever After High, remember?"

"Exactly! So enchant us! When we get to the courtyard, biggify us, just like you biggify your pet dragon. We'll pick up the Zomboyz and carry them to the bridge."

"Nevermore gets big by her own power," Raven says. The imaginary dragon rubs against Raven's ankles like a cat. "And it's dangerous to biggify people. Magical animals take it the best. Baba Yaga said she tried it on a regular old beetle once, and the poor thing hexploded."

"Oh." Frankie sighs. She had been so certain her plan would work. But that was silly.

Draculaura popped into bat form. "Biggify *me*," she squeaked. "Magical animal, at your service."

"Ladies," a familiar voice calls from the courtyard, "so...*interesting* to see you here." Moanica D'Kay's wedge heels clack as she walks across the stone ground. She bends to pick up a dirty sneaker and holds it between her thumb and forefinger as if it were someone else's used tissue. "Zomboyz. Always losing things, amirite? Shoes. Limbs. Card games."

"Moanica!" Draculaura calls out. "What are you doing? Why are you even part of this?"

Moanica smiles. "It's fun," she says, advancing through the crowd of Zomboyz.

"Fun?" Frankie shouts. "Your sorceress friend is going to destroy the world!"

"Not *our* world," Moanica says. "I get to be empress of ours. She promised. Finally somebody who gets me!"

Moanica drops the dirty shoe by the barefoot Zomboy.

"*Uhhh.*" The Zomboy groans, grabbing at the sneaker.

Nevermore, hovering at the wall of fog, snaps at Moanica. She flinches, but Nevermore doesn't go after her.

"Why can't your little friend come any closer?" she asks. "Could it be that *my* friend's magic is stronger than *your* friend's magic?"

Moanica takes a step onto the bridge. Little Nevermore snaps again, but Moanica ignores her. She bumps into Moanica, and the zombie girl bats her away.

"Silly Zomboyz," Moanica says. "They scare so easily."

Nevermore enlarges to full size and roars. Moanica's eyes widen, but she doesn't run.

"That *is* scarier," she says, and then takes another tentative step. The large dragon snaps at her, but Moanica pushes her muzzle away. The Zomboyz follow behind Moanica, groaning after everything she says, as if in agreement.

Nevermore sits angrily on the bridge, her bulk preventing Moanica from moving any closer. The zombie girl pushes at the dragon to no effect. "I wonder…" Moanica mutters. She takes a step, slipping on the bridge and careening over the edge.

"No!" Raven yells. Nevermore darts to the girl to catch her, but she has already caught the edge of the bridge and pulled herself up.

"So…you don't want to hurt me," Moanica says. "You don't want to hurt any of us."

"Of course not," Apple says. "We're not *monsters*." She blushes, glancing sideways at Frankie and Draculaura. "Well, um, some of us are…"

Moanica waves her Zomboyz forward. "Come on, boys, climb over the dragon. If you fall, she'll save you."

"Uh-oh," Frankie says.

Draculaura pops into bat form. "How long does it take you to cast the biggify spell?" she whispers to Raven.

"Not long," she says. "Like a second. But I can't do it in the fog."

All the Zomboyz have crowded onto the bridge. One Zomboy, crawling over the dragon, slips and tips into the lava-bottomed fog. But the dragon catches the boy with a claw and places him back on the bridge.

Frankie takes a breath. She has an idea. She doesn't like that she has this particular idea, but it's there, pressing against the inside of her skull, falling onto her tongue.

"We could ride the dragon," Frankie whispers.

"The *imaginary* dragon?" Apple asks.

"Everybody on the imaginary dragon!" Dracu-laura says.

"Wait…what if this isn't a good plan?" says Frankie.

"It's your plan," says Draculaura. "How could it not be good?"

Apple, Frankie, and Raven pile on the imaginary dragon as Bat-Drac zips to the courtyard over the heads of the Zomboyz.

As the dragon rises, Frankie can't help looking down. Her stomach feels full of dust moths. If she tumbles off, she won't just fall to pieces—she'll fall into lava. *Poof*—no more Frankie.

"You can't fool me," Moanica calls from below. "I see my little bat-friend Draculaura headed toward the library, but I'm not worried about her. Your mother made it clear that you are the one I need to keep out, Raven Queen."

"What are we going to do?" Apple asks.

The dragon flaps her imaginary wings, and they rise.

"We're going in," Raven says.

Moanica and the Zomboyz are so far below they look like miniature versions of themselves.

"I'm scared." Frankie turns to Apple, who is

clutching Nevermore's saddle so tightly her hands are trembling. "Are you scared?"

Apple makes a little *eep* noise.

"Is Raven crazy?" Frankie whispers.

Apple shakes her head once to indicate *no*, and then the dragon speeds through the wall of fog and hovers high above the courtyard.

"Huh," Apple says. "I thought Nevermore would disappear the second we passed through the fog. Maybe—"

Suddenly, they are sitting on nothing.

They fall. Frankie takes a deep breath. It is going to hurt when she hits stone, but at least it's not lava. Apple has taken a deep breath, too, but she is using it to scream. Then Frankie realizes…Apple is a *Normie*. Or mostly a Normie. If she falls apart, she can't be sewn together again. Frankie pinwheels her arms, reaching for Apple and pulls her into a hug. She closes her eyes, hoping her body will be enough of a cushion to save Apple.

She does not expect to be plucked from the air by a giant bat claw and placed softly on the stones of the courtyard.

"*Yes!*" says Raven. "I did it! Speed magic! Good work, Draculaura!"

"Good work, Raven!" Draculaura's embiggened bat form is at least as huge as Nevermore was. She lifts a massive wing and slaps it against Raven's uplifted palm.

"Whoa," Apple whispers, staring at the solid rock beneath her. "Frankie, were you trying to save my life?"

"Trying," admits Frankie.

"Thanks," says Apple. "That was fairy brave. And fairy nice."

"*Woo-hoo!*" shouts Big Bat-Drac, doing a loop-the-loop and then diving at the Zomboyz. She plucks Zomboyz from the ground two by two, flies them a hundred feet back along the bridge, and drops them off. She gets Moanica last.

"Let me go, you giant leather-winged monster!" Moanica yells.

So Draculaura lets her go, far, far down the bridge.

Bat-Drac returns, landing beside Frankie with a rush of wind. "It will take them a minute or so to walk back," she says.

"Hold on," Raven says, tracing a pattern in the air. Bat-Drac is enveloped in a green glow and quickly shrinks to her normal size.

"Aw, man," Draculaura squeaks, popping back into human form. "That was too fun."

"I had to get you back to normal before you turned human," Raven says. "Or vampire. Whatever. I'm just not sure what would have happened. Might have been dangerous."

"Dangerous?" Frankie asks. "Like flying us scary high before dropping us to our doom? I might have been okay, but poor Apple? She could have gotten hurt!"

"I'm really sorry," Raven says. "I needed as much falling time as possible to make sure I could cast the biggify spell on Drac."

"I wouldn't have let you fall," Draculaura says with a reassuring smile. "Let's go, Raven. I'll be your backup." The two of them hurry toward the library.

"The Zomboyz are coming back," Frankie says, peering at the bridge. "Moanica is faster than the rest of them."

"What's next, Frankie?" asks Apple.

"You're asking me?" Frankie says. "Oh, right, this was my plan. We've switched places. Okay." She gulps. "We need ... to step into the fog and imagine a wall. A big wall they can't climb, to keep them on the bridge."

Apple takes another step into the Margins, and a beautiful picket fence springs up and then vanishes. "Wait," she says. "Drac said we'd be okay as long as Moanica wasn't here. She's here."

"Bolts!" Frankie says. "You're right. She'll figure out that she can do the imagination thing, too."

"She didn't know Nevermore was imaginary," Apple says. "She thought it was Raven's magic. Maybe we can—"

"You can't do anything!" Moanica shouts at them, marching through the fog. "A sorceress and a vampire might have had a chance against us, but what are you? A science geek without a lab and a...whatever you are. What are you, anyway?"

A spark fires in Frankie's brain. "Wait, you don't know who she is?"

"She's nobody," Moanica says, though she doesn't look sure. "Some goofy fairytale."

"This is *the* Fairy Queen," Frankie proclaims, gesturing grandly at Apple, who, after a moment of hesitation, curtsies.

"You're making that up," Moanica says. "You always talk a little louder than normal when you're lying. Did you know that?"

"I was proclaiming," Frankie says, louder still.

Apple prances forward, attempting to play her part. "Perhaps what you perceive, dear girl, is the hexcess of honor young Frankie gives me. For I am not yet the queen; I am but a princess."

"I guess that makes sense," Moanica says. "But who cares? My 'boyz can capture a fairy princess just as easily as a normal one."

"What if," Frankie says, gritting her teeth in concentration, "the princess commands a fairy army?"

Two small figures appear above Apple. They have buzzing dragonfly wings and barbarian warrior garb; each grips a two-inch ax.

Moanica starts at the sudden appearance and then laughs. "*That* is your fairy army, Princess? Two floating dolls?"

Apple looks at Frankie and nods. Frankie closes her eyes and tries to imagine as many fairy warriors as she can.

"Hardly," Apple says, holding up her arms in a way she has seen the Evil Queen do. "This is my army!"

Nothing happens.

"Um…" Moanica says.

Frankie tries to forget she is on a bridge in the middle of nowhere. She tells herself a story about Apple as a true Fairy Queen going to battle against a vast evil army.

"Oh," Apple says, and Frankie opens her eyes. Apple's clothing has changed from her red-and-gold skirt and white blouse into a shining suit of crystal armor, and buzzing in from the sky on either side of the bridge are hundreds of warrior-fairies.

"Ha!" Apple shouts, getting back into character. "Charge! Drive them back, my brave soldiers!"

The imaginary fairy army dives at the Zomboyz. Half of them turn and run, and the other half, too slow to understand what is happening, begin getting poked and prodded by tiny weapons. Moanica shouts, swatting at fairies.

"Real fairies don't look anything like that," Apple whispers to Frankie.

"Hopefully, Moanica doesn't know the difference," Frankie says.

"*Ow!*" Moanica shouts, batting at a fairy poking her with a sharp stick. "Get back, you flying thumb!"

"I like your fairies better," Apple whispers. "But don't tell the real ones I said that."

CHAPTER 20

ND SO WHAT HAPPENS NEXT IS... RAVEN AND Draculaura follow the compass into a cellar, Raven uses magical energy to move stones out of the way and release Maddie, and then Raven and Maddie hug and take the time to say how happy they are to see each other, *even though* they're wasting precious seconds while the Evil Queen is upstairs doing something terrible that might destroy the world! *Ahem!*[63]

"Thanks for the rescuing," says Maddie, "but

---

63 Sorry, I'm getting a little impatient. But why do characters take so long when there's a crisis? Hurry up!

our Narrator is insisting we hurry and deal with your mom quick-quick," which isn't technically true, because Narrators would never *make* someone do something they wouldn't otherwise do.

"Drac, can you take Maddie and get her safe?" asks Raven. "I'll stay and—"

"Wait, you want us to leave?" asks Draculaura.

"Maddie's been locked up and needs—"

"I don't need anything," says Maddie. "I'm peachy. Peach cobblery, even. With whipped cream on top."

So much talking, not enough hurrying!

"Sorry, Brooke," says Maddie.

"You don't have to do this alone, Raven," Draculaura says. "Remember when we fought your imaginary mothers in the fog? We did it together."

"*Ooh*, I've missed so much!" says Maddie.

"But this isn't imaginary!" protests Raven. "This is the real thing! This is really her! And...and you don't know her, Drac. She's...she's..."

"The *Eee-vil* Queen!" Maddie says ominously, wiggling her fingers in a spooky manner. "With a spray bottle!"

"Well, last time all we had was an imaginary

Maddie to help us," Draculaura says. "Now we've got the real thing!"

"Tarn dootin'!" Maddie says. "Real like fish and twice as slippery!"

Raven can't help but smile.

Aaaand...now is the part when they start to hurry, probably. *Aaaany* second now. Ready, set—

"Go!" says Maddie. "We should go!"

The girls run up the stairs and through the library, climbing over piles of rubble, crossing floors of ancient tile mosaics, around tilty bookshelves— some empty, some with scattered tomes. They follow the sound of chanting.

At last they reach a room that's only half a room, really. Part of a tiled roof balances above, and the three remaining walls are lined with bookshelves. The missing wall is open to the outside, the huge hole like the gaping mouth of a whale, loose stones and dangling roof tiles like its teeth. The Evil Queen is standing in the mouth-that's-not-really-a-mouth-just-a-hole-in-the-wall, facing the...basically the shore of the library's island.[64]

---

64 Sorry, Reader, this is not my best sentence. It's just all so tense!

She chants:

> Draw back the key,
> pluck out the pin,
> pull forth that debris
> feared by Brooke's kin.

A rope of twined black and silver magic extends out of the fog, and as the Evil Queen chants, she tugs on the magic rope as if pulling something closer.

What is she pulling toward herself?[65]

Raven tiptoes nearer and thrusts her hands out. A current of purple light zaps toward the Evil Queen. Without turning around, the queen waves her hand, knocking the purple zap away. Instantly, a dome of transparent silvery magic rolls down and around the Evil Queen, cutting her off from the girls.

"Oh no," says Raven. "She had a shield spell ready, contingent on any magical attack."

"*Ooh*, you should do that, too," suggests Draculaura.

---

65 I think my parents know, but they can't tell me because they are seriously *flipping out* and can't even talk coherently, and when they're flipping out this badly, it makes me panic, too. Hey, Evil Queen, whatever you're doing, I think it's both literally and figuratively *evil*.

"That's really advanced magic," says Raven. "I'm still in high school."

Raven sends bolts of purple magic at the shield, but they bounce off like balloons.

"Raven, sweetheart, my own little dumpling, you found your mama!" calls the Evil Queen from inside the magical dome shield.

After she speaks, the Evil Queen's lips keep moving, as if she's continuing the spell's chant under her breath. And she keeps pulling on that magical rope, too, hand over hand, steady and determined.

"I don't know what's going on, Mother," says Raven, "but—"

"Your power has grown," says the Evil Queen, examining the hand she used to bat away Raven's spell, as if checking for injury. "How delightful! I knew you'd take more after your majestic and awe-inspiring mother than that father of yours. The 'Good' King. *Boooring!* But, my sweet little Black Forest cake, you can't win. I simply know more than you do. I've had more time. And with these books here, I've learned things no one else has known since ancient times."

"Can you open a hole in her barrier, Raven?"

Draculaura whispers. "Just big enough for a tiny bat to get through?"

"Maybe, but, Drac…I won't be able to big-gify you behind that shield. What would you do to stop her?"

Draculaura pulls the Skullette on its chain from under her shirt. "This is humming again. Your mom must have the Monster Mapalogue near, and maybe between that and being out of the fog, it's recharged. If I get close enough to touch her, it could send us both back to Monster High."

Yes, good idea. Draculaura has a good idea. Any idea is good, because if the Evil Queen succeeds with whatever she is attempting, the consequences will be apocalyptic.[66]

Maddie raises her hand. "Mrs. Queen?"

The Evil Queen laughs. "I know it feels like you're being taken to school, Ms. Hatter, but no need to raise hands. Show some pluck. Stand your ground and shout your demands at the world!"

"*Okay!*" says Maddie. "*I am now shouting at the world! And at you specifically!* So, uh, you wanted to

---

66 At least, that's my guess. None of the other Narrators can stop panicking long enough to explain it to me!

know what the Narrators were saying, right? Well, one of them is saying whatever it is you're doing is apoplectic."

"Hexcuse me?"

"No, wait. Apologetic. It's apologetic."

"Ah. I think the word you're looking for is *apocalyptic*," says the dark sorceress. "As in, something that will cause the complete destruction of the world. And for the Narrators, I suppose what I'm doing *is* apocalyptic. Because once I reach Shadow High and claim the power of the Narrators, they will lose their power and won't be able to rule us anymore. Honestly, Raven, who would you rather have controlling your life? Invisible beings who never show or name themselves, or your dear, beautiful, intelligent, powerful mother?"

Raven doesn't answer. Her eyes are closed, her forehead beaded with sweat; her lips mumble something, and then a fist-size hole opens in the shield.

Pop! Draculaura turns into a bat and swooshes through the hole, diving straight for the Evil Queen. But before she can change to her natural form, the Evil Queen grabs her by the Skullette pendant around her neck, yanks it off, and, with a brush of her hand, sends the Bat-Drac tumbling back through the hole. The shield seals shut.

"Aha! I thought a piece of my Mapalogue was missing," says the Evil Queen. "So kind of you to have a winged rat deliver it to me."

Pop! Draculaura sits on the ground and rubs the back of her neck. "Not cool. Not cool at all."

The Evil Queen continues to mumble and pull on the rope of magic.

Raven touches the glowing surface of the shield. It feels like soft glass.

"What if you're wrong?" Raven asks. "What if we need Narrators to tell our stories? What if we need Narrators to exist at all?"

The Evil Queen turns to look fully at her daughter, an inch of nearly transparent energy between them. They both appear to be looking into a mirror, one side showing the future, the other the past.

"That's your fear talking," the Evil Queen says. "This is my fight for control, control of our *own* destiny."

"Then let me have my destiny, whatever it is. Don't break the world before I can find my own path!"

"You can't, my little semiprecious stone," the Evil Queen coos. "You never could. I'm beginning to believe that the terrible secret of all this is that we have no real control at all—not as long as there are Narrators."

That's not true! That's not true at all![67]

"Not true, not true!" says Maddie.

"The Narrators shape destiny, Raven," says the Evil Queen, ignoring Maddie and still hauling in that magical tether. "They control us. We need to take that back. All I've ever wanted is to control my own destiny. They called me *evil* because I decided not to follow a script and instead make bold, magical, kingdom-shaking choices! Tell me, is it evil to simply try to control your own life?"

"No, Mom. But it *is* evil to want to control other people's lives."

"Yeah!" says Draculaura. "That's right! You tell her, Raven."

The Evil Queen shifts her gaze to Draculaura, who scoots backward.

"Draculaura, daughter of Dracula, cofounder of Monster High. I know *you* understand me."

---

67 It's *not* true. I'm sure she read some really smart books and all, but the Evil Queen is totally misinterpreting them!

Draculaura gulps. "I do?"

"I'm fighting to bring the pieces of our world together," she says. "Isn't that what you are working toward with your school? To bring the monsters out of hiding? To first unify the monsters and then one day, hopefully, the monster and Normie worlds? Through my reading in this very library, I have learned that once upon a time, all our lands were unified. Your ancestors and mine were possibly friends! And then the Narrators broke us apart, out of fear. Fear of *us*. Fear that we would work together to defeat them. We're all just characters in a story to them, Draculaura. It's time for us to be *people*."

"Oh," says Draculaura, nodding as if she can't help it.

Even Raven feels wooed by the words. Could it be her mother is speaking the truth?[68]

"Is that true, Brooke?" Maddie asks. "Am I not a people? I always thought I was a people."

Um...the Narrator needs to tell what's happening in the story, not answer characters' questions.

"Characters?" asks Maddie. "You mean us?"

---

68 I...I don't *think* this is true. But I'm not sure. Did the lands all used to be together? Were the Narrators responsible for breaking it apart?

Yes, but…but that's who you are. You're characters in the story of your lives. That doesn't mean you're not people, too. I think. The other Narrators here are still panicking too much to explain it to me, but some of what the Evil Queen said sounds kinda true.

"I'm so confusal in my noodle," says Maddie.

"Mom, please," says Raven.

Her mother sighs. "I want what's best for you, Raven. Always."

The Evil Queen puts one of her hands up and presses it to her daughter's. The shield between them flickers and vanishes.

"Thanks, Mom," says Raven.

The Evil Queen raises an arched eyebrow. "Whatever for?"

Raven stutters a laugh, gesturing around her. "For dropping the barrier. For stopping what you were doing. For seeing reason. For being on my side."

From somewhere in the distance comes a rumble, low and trembly and growing louder.

"I hear a critter," Maddie whispers. "A *big*

critter that is hungry maybe for peachy cobbler with whipped cream."

"That's no critter." The Evil Queen looks out. "Raven, I am always on your side, because we're on the *same* side, my precious lump of coal. But I haven't stopped. I've *finished*. That foggy wilderness you walked through is called the Margins. The place between stories. The space keeping all the lands apart. And the rumbling you hear is the Margins narrowing. It is the sound of the Narrators' great secret being pulled toward us."

"No," Raven whispers.

"Now I just need the last piece...."

Loosen the key,
free the key,
at last, at last the key to me!

The Evil Queen gives the magical rope a hard yank.

An object streaks out of the fog like an arrow, the end of the rope tied around its middle. Just before it strikes the queen in the face, she plucks it easily from the air as if it weren't moving at the speed of a falling star. She turns it over, her brow wrinkled.

"*Hmm,*" she says. "I'll be honest. I'm a little surprised." She speaks upward, as if to people in the sky. "And disappointed! This is the great key I read about in ancient books? The magical object you Narrators used to lock in place Shadow High's island from the rest of the world? No flair for drama, you people! I hexpected the object would be a sword or an electric disk or, good heavens, an actual *key*!"

"What is it?" Raven asks.

The Evil Queen holds up the flat plank of iron, vaguely triangular and pockmarked with age.

"It's a chisel," Raven says.

"So it would seem," says the Evil Queen, unimpressed. She begins to pace, closer to the edge of the island. Raven follows.

"Combined with some spell, this chisel is what locked Shadow High away for so long," says the Evil Queen. "And kept the other lands away from it. Well, no longer is Shadow High stuck, pinned down by the ancient magic of this chisel. I don't have to go to Shadow High. It is, even now, coming to *me*."

And in the distance, the groaning of the critter that isn't a critter grows louder. Hungrier. Nearer.[69]

---

69 A critter that eats peach cobbler would be *so much better* than what's actually coming!

CHAPTER 21

RAVEN STEPS OUT FROM BENEATH THE CRUMBLING roof of the library. She feels Maddie and Draculaura follow. They stare into the fog. Something is out there.

"What is that?" says Draculaura. "A mountain?"

The mountain—or whatever—is slowly advancing, sailing like a ship through the foggy Margins and directly toward them.

"*Spooooky* mountain," says Maddie.

"I like spooky mountains," says Draculaura, "but I do *not* like that."

"I get you," Raven says. "I mean, why am I scared?"

"Because you're a smart girl," Draculaura says, "and smart girls know to be scared of dark, mysterious mountains sailing like boats through foggy, mysterious places."

"Oh, right," says Raven.

"That is not a mountain," says the Evil Queen. "That's an island. And on that island is Shadow High. Forgive me, girls, but I must... I must... *MWAHAHAHA!*" She laughs a loud, mother-goosebump-y evil laugh. "Sorry, I know it's a cliché, but it had to be done."

The color of the air is changing. Raven looks up. Is a sun showing its face through the fog? No, the orangey glow is coming from below. As the Shadow High island nears, the trench between the two islands is narrowing, and the lava that bubbled down deep is slowly rising up.

The new island is so close now that a black structure is visible through the haze—a flat-topped mountain.[70]

The Evil Queen isn't saying *MWAHAHA* anymore, but she can't seem to stop herself from performing

---

70 Oh, I see—it's a *volcano*.

a very un-evil-like hoppity dance. Maddie nods approvingly. Of the hoppity dance, that is.

The Evil Queen is on the very edge of the island, looking over. She picks up the spray bottle she threw onto a pile of bricks and drops it off the island.

But whatever the Evil Queen sees happen to the spray bottle down below takes the smile right off her face and the hoppity out of her feet.

"Mother?" asks Raven. "What's going on?"

"Oh bubble parties," the Evil Queen says. "Bunny eyelashes and rainbow sprinkles. Hot chocolate and fish kites. *Oh, skipping to Grandmother's house!*"[71]

"Is she casting a spell?" Draculaura whispers.

"No, she's…uh, she's swearing," says Raven. "The things most people consider nice are bad words to her."[72]

A small wave of lava rises up and washes over the edge of the island, splashing on one of the fallen books. Raven expects the book to catch fire and scorch, but apparently this isn't your normal superhot, melty-rock, run-of-the-mill volcano lava. Instead, when the lava touches it, the substance of the

71 Um…no idea what she's saying here, TBH.
72 Oh, okay. Weird, but okay.

book itself is wiped away, leaving behind just a book skeleton made of words: S P I N E, C O V E R, P A G E, P A G E, P A G E, P A G E, P A G E…

When the small wave of lava recedes back over the edge of the island, all that remains is a jumble of words in the shape of what was once a book.

The Evil Queen bends over, and at the touch of her finger, the stacked letters crumble into a heap and blow away.

"No…" the Evil Queen whispers. "The Unmaking. That's what that old book was talking about. *Unmaking lava.* I didn't understand.…"

"What are you saying?" asks Raven.

There's something in her mother's eyes Raven has never seen before. Fear. The Evil Queen is actually afraid. Raven's gut seems to turn to ice and fall into her shoes. And from down in her shoes, her gut assures her that if the Evil Queen is afraid, then everyone should be.

The Evil Queen is squinting at the island mountain moving slowly through the Margins. She takes a deep breath and pushes her hands out in front of her. Two beams of purple magic shoot from her hands, pierce the fog, and strike the oncoming island.

"I...I was wrong," says the Evil Queen. "The power of Shadow High. This situation. It's not...not what I...what I thought."

"Push the land back, Mother!" Raven shouts.

"I'm trying!"

Raven joins her, hands out, both of them shooting streams of magic. The island slows only slightly.

The Evil Queen shouts and then falls back, her face damp with sweat. When her magic beams cease, the island jolts forward.

"Nothing!" she says. "That did nothing! No force of magic can stop it."

"Is she going to start 'swearing' again?" whispers Maddie. "'Cause that was funny."

"Um, it did *something*," says Draculaura. "Look."

When the island jolted forward, a second shape rose up in the fog, even closer to them than the volcano on the island.

"Another mountain?" guesses Draculaura.

"That's no mountain," the Evil Queen says. "That's a wave."

"Of *lava*?" asks Raven. "A wave of lava? Of that same lava that just took apart a book?"

"I *have* always wanted to try surfing," Maddie

says. "But that does not look like a beginner wave. I think we need to dash like rabbits who are running late."

"Yes," the Evil Queen agrees. "Run."

Raven grabs Maddie's hand and turns back toward the library. "C'mon, Drac!" she yells. Ahead of them, Raven's mother has picked up her skirts and is vaulting over fallen stones and threading through the labyrinth of bookcases. Raven can't help looking back as she runs. The wave is closer.

"The approach of Shadow High is pushing the lava up toward us," says Raven. "You have to stop that island, Mother!"

"These lands were once all part of the same continent," her mother yells back. "When I pulled loose the magic chisel from Shadow High's island, it freed the island's power. It's the center of the world. All the lands, including this one, are being pulled toward Shadow High like metal filings to a magnet."

"So put the chisel back!" shouts Raven. "Redo the spell that turned off its magnet power or whatever, and keep the lands apart!"

"Oh, okay, I'll just do that, then. Why didn't I

think of that genius plan first? Oh yes, because it's *impossible*!"

They clear the library and run across the island toward the bridge, where Frankie and Apple appear to be battling the remaining Zomboyz and Moanica with an army of flying dolls.

"Apple!" Raven yells. "Frankie!"

Just as the girls turn to look at Raven, some lava bubbles up over the shore, a stream of orange-gold that cuts off the edge of the bridge from the island. Apple yelps and leaps off the bridge and over the stream of lava to the island. The sparkly armor she was wearing disappears. Frankie follows, but she leaps a little farther. When Apple lands, one of her shoes touches the lava. It breaks down into words: H E E L, A R C H, B U C K L E, S O L E...

"*Eep!*" squeaks Apple, stepping out of the shoe that is now just a stack of letters. "That is *not* my story," she says disapprovingly to her lost shoe. "But...how did that happen?"

"Hexplain later!" says Raven. "Now we run.... Um, where do we run?"

The enormous wave of lava is so close they can feel the oncoming breeze of its speed.

"Oh my corpse," says Moanica, backing away from the pooling lava that now separates the bridge from the gathered group of girls on the land. "Come on, Zomboyz. Let's get back to Monster High!"

The undead crew runs/shambles up the arching bridge and deeper into the fog of the Margins.

"Frankie, that bridge could take us back to Monster High," says Draculaura.

Frankie glances at Apple. "You go, Drac. Follow the bridge and fly home. I'm going to stay and try to help fix this. It's my fault."

"It's not your fault, Frankie," says Draculaura. But she doesn't change into a bat and fly away.

Another slosh of lava rises up on the shore, forming a wide pool between them and the bridge to Monster High.

"We're trapped," Raven says.

"There's another bridge," declares the Evil Queen. "Follow me or perish!"

"Sheesh, Mother, do you always have to be so dramatic?" says Raven.

"Uh, Raven?" Apple pipes up, running beside her with a lopsided gait, one foot bare. "When we're fleeing a wave of lava on an island in the middle of a foggy wilderness where imagination takes form, saying dramatic things isn't entirely out of place."

"Okay, good point," says Raven.

Up ahead, another bridge arches away from the island. The Evil Queen reaches it first. The girls follow; Raven is the last to enter the fog of the Margins.

Or almost last. She looks back to see that Apple has tripped on her remaining shoe. The wave of lava has begun to roll over the island, a hundred feet of bright orange and gold. Before it falls, Raven leaps from the bridge back onto the island.

"Raven, no!" shouts the Evil Queen.

But Raven knows she must be on the island to use her magic. She lifts her hands, creating a shield, a purple wall to stop the tide of lava.

It holds for two seconds before the shield breaks apart into thousands of letters spelling over and over again: RAVENSUSELESSSHIELD...

"Now, that's just rude," says Raven.

Apple is back on her feet and they run for the bridge, the crashing wave nearly upon them.

But it stops again, held by a second shield. The Evil Queen has stepped off the bridge.

"Hurry, fools!" she shouts.

Her shield lasts only seconds longer before bursting into a storm of letters.

But it's enough. They manage to run up the slope of the bridge as the wave crashes behind them. Raven turns in time to see the lava drench the ruined library, flooding its crumbling chambers. As the lava recedes, it leaves behind a library-shaped structure completely made out of words.

L I B R A R Y, L I B R A R Y, L I B R A R Y, LIBRARY, LIBRARY...

As Raven peers closer, she realizes the large letters are made up of even smaller letters: S P I R E, W I N D O W, W A L L, B R I C K, B O O K, B O O K, B O O K, B O O K...

The white stone of the island itself is not unmade, remaining solid under the splashing and sploshing lava. But the lava never fully recedes. The low-lying island stays almost entirely underwater—or under-lava, so to speak.

And the Shadow High island is so close that if Raven could stand on the library island, she could probably leap from one island to the next and discover for herself what awaits there.

The fog of the Margins is as thick as an ogre's

breath. Raven hugs her arms around herself and shivers. Through the fog, she can see the outline of the great black building in the middle of that island. The shape reminds her of Ever After High. It's a school—it's definitely a school.

Shadow High.

CHAPTER 22

WAIT A SENTENCE! THIS HAS GONE FAR ENOUGH. Mom. Dad. I need to know. What is that lava? Why is the world in pieces? What is Shadow High?

AAAH!

Can you please—

AAAH!

…stop flipping out long enough—

AAAAH!

…to explain it to me?

Whew. Ugh. Bleh. Okay. You're right, Brooke. Sorry. It's time. This history is so dangerous, Narrators usually learn about it only after they've graduated from Narrator High.

But you should know now, Brooke, even though it might already be too late to stop what's happening. Once upon a time, long, long ago, in the land of Readers, the First Author made up the very first story. She used a chisel to inscribe the story in stone. It was such a good story that people kept reading it and retelling it. And that awakened a kind of magic.

The best kind of magic! The characters in that story came to life! Not in the Readers' World, but across the Fourth Wall in the World of Stories. And as the centuries marched on, whenever the Readers told and retold stories, their characters came to life. Soon the World of Stories was full of characters— and their children, and their children's children.

Each character lived in the land devoted to his or her kind of story. There was a land of adventure stories—pirates and ninjas and explorers traveling through new places. There was a land of science-fiction stories—rocket ships and outer space and adventures with aliens!

There was a land of mythological stories—gods and goddesses meddling with human matters, ancient creatures crawling out of deep pits. There were lands of holiday stories, romance stories, superhero stories, epic fantasy stories, mystery stories, Wonderland stories—

And...I guess there were lands of monster stories and fairytale stories?

That's right. They were all together in one big, beautiful World of Stories. And it was the Narrators' job to keep telling the stories of the characters in this world. Some Narrators believed the characters should keep living out the same stories the Readers first wrote down, and some Narrators believed characters should be free to live their lives however they chose. I'm one of the former; your father is one of the latter.

But there was a third kind of Narrator. She called herself Ms. Direction. She believed that the Narrators should have more power, that they should decide what happened in the stories. So she founded a school to teach other Narrators her way. They learned how to not just narrate what characters were doing but to also force the characters to do what the Narrators wanted them to do.

Shadow High…

That's right, Brooke. To control the stories, these Narrators created a magic that unmade the stories, breaking them down to bits, believing that they could then take the pieces and build new stories. Ms. Direction was powerful, but even she couldn't control what she had begun. The Unmaking magic erupted like lava from a volcano. First it unmade her school, and then it began to flow all over the World of Stories, unmaking everything it touched.

In order to stop the flow of the Unmaking lava, the rest of the Narrators had to break all the rules. First they sought out and retrieved the chisel that the First Author had used to write the First Story. It was an object of great power. Then one brave Narrator volunteered to leave the Land of Narrators and journey into the World of Stories to Shadow High. He used all the power of the Narrators and the characters to enchant the chisel with a great magic. When he hammered the chisel into Shadow High, the spell broke the world.

The different lands cracked and moved away from one another, becoming continents and islands. Now the Unmaking that was flowing from the volcano at Shadow High could fall harmlessly into the trenches of the Margins, the spaces between the lands.

The World of Stories would be safe as long as it stayed broken and the lands separate from one another. That Narrator sacrificed his own life to hammer that chisel into Shadow High's island, keeping it still and away from the other lands at the center of the World of Stories.

Narrators tried to erase all references to Shadow High from books. As the years passed, most characters didn't know that the World of Stories had ever been unified. They assumed the stories about other lands were just made-up tales. But when the characters from Ever After High and Monster High began to reach out to one another, the lands started to shift, to feel that pull to reconnect.

That caused the tremors.

Exactly. And when the Evil Queen found the Lost Library and got very near Shadow High, a fail-safe in the ancient spell caused the World of Stories to break again, this time into even smaller pieces. And so the Margins reached right up to the edge of Ever After High.

The Evil Queen found an ancient book that the Narrators couldn't erase. It mentioned a powerful "key" holding Shadow High away from other lands, and she used her magic to pull it loose. Now that Shadow High is free from the spell of the chisel, it is indeed like a magnet, pulling all the lands together again.

The Margins are narrowing. The Unmaking is rising in the trenches between the lands. Soon it will flow over all the lands as it did over the Lost Library. If we can't stop it, the entire World of Stories will be unmade.

Wait, Dad, do you mean that nowhere is safe? But what about over the Fourth Wall?

In the Readers' World? Characters cannot live there. No one from the World of Stories could make that journey.

There's still hope! I may not have graduated yet

from Narrator High, but I know a lot of stories, and I can see how this one goes. It's an adventure story, with both mystery and magic. The group of characters—two monsters, two daughters of fairy-tales, one child of Wonderland, plus an evil villain—must travel to the mysterious and dangerous Shadow High and replace the chisel. Once the chisel is back, the lands will stop coming together and the Unmaking lava will stay safe down in the trenches between lands. I'd better tell the others.

Well, we already have. At least, I'm pretty certain Madeline Hatter has been eavesdropping on this entire conversation.

Yessiree, Bob's your uncle! Whew! There was a lot of information in this chapter.

Hi, Maddie! Yeah, it was pretty information-heavy. Narrators call it *exposition*.

Well, I call it a head-scratcher. World of Stories? First chisel? Ms. Direction? There's just too much going on! But I think I got the basics: Find Shadow High. Put back the chisel. Save the world. Right?

You got it, Maddie.

Okay, I'll tell Raven and Apple and everyone what you said. Though I may add a few jokes. Jokes make everything better. Even news about how the entire world is going to end unless we hurry over foggy, mysterious bridges to an evil island and find some kind of a hole? To put a chisel in? And somehow that will fix everything?

I like knock-knock jokes best.

Hey, Brooke? Knock, knock.

Who's there?

Interrupting Narrator.

Interrupting Narrator wh—

AAAH EVERYBODY IS PANICKING HURRY WITH CHISELS BLAAAAAAAGHHH!!!

Good one, Maddie.

Thanks, Brooke!

CHAPTER 23

THE MARGINS. THAT IS WHAT THE EVIL QUEEN and Maddie said the fog parts are called. Now that Frankie knows what it is, she scans the fog as she goes, studying it, eager to understand it. The space between "stories." Between lands. The Margins is a place where new stories, new universes, might one day come to exist. Fascinating! She peeks over the edge of the bridge they're walking on. The lava is higher than it was an hour ago. Scary! Fascinating…but also scary! So many emotions that the ends of her hair frizzle and her fingernails buzz.

Ahead, through the mist, Frankie spots another

fork in the bridge. She hooks the wire powering the compass back to her bolts and turns the contraption on. Now, instead of Maddie's teacup, the chisel is fitted in the compass's spinning mechanism. The gears grind as the device spins. She didn't build it to hold something as heavy as the chisel, and she worries the compass will break. But so far it's holding, and the glowy green arrow points them to the right fork of the bridge. The way to Shadow High.

There go her goosebumps again.

After directing the group to the right, she powers down the compass and watches the chisel's spin slow to a stop.

"I don't understand," she says. "How can a little chisel be big enough to anchor down an entire island, let alone keep all the lands of the world apart?"

"How can a little key be big enough to open a large door?" asks the Evil Queen, walking beside Frankie, always one step ahead. "Or an acorn big enough to grow an oak tree? Why, you don't even think twice when overnight a magic bean becomes a beanstalk that carries you to the land of giants in the clouds."

"*I* would think twice," Frankie mumbles.

"Wait…that beanstalk thing doesn't really happen, does it?" asks Draculaura.

"No way. It makes no scientific sense," says Frankie. "Besides, how would a big, heavy giant walk on clouds without falling through?"

Maddie laughs. "Hah! I love you guys! Next you'll be asking how puppets can talk!"

The Evil Queen ignores them. "Small things do great things all the time. Just look at me." The Evil Queen bats her eyelashes and puts her hands coyly beneath her chin. "Would you ever believe that *sweet little me* would one day rule the entire world?"

"Nope," Maddie says cheerfully.

The Evil Queen glares daggers at her.

Maddie frowns. "Oops, was that one of those 'there's only one right answer' quizzes? I prefer oral reports."

Frankie shoots a glance at Draculaura to see if she's remembering their failed class presentation, and how it was all Frankie's fault. But Draculaura is ambling along beside Raven and chatting like they're old friends. Frankie sighs.

"You walk in front now," the Evil Queen tells Frankie, falling back into step with Raven. "I'm tired of hearing that disgusting wheezing noise next to me. It makes my skin crawl."

Frankie shivers again but scolds herself for it. In the Margins, the Evil Queen's magic is gone. Technically, she is just a grumpy lady in an extravagant outfit. And perfect makeup. Also she is pretty tall. But she is still scary. Fascinating! . . . But scary.

"You mean *breathing*, Mother?" Raven says. "You don't like hearing Frankie *breathe*?"

"Oh, don't be tedious," the queen says. "I don't like hearing *any* of you breathe."

"Maybe she needs earplugs," Maddie mutters to Raven. Then, yelling at the queen, *"Maybe you need earplugs!"*

"I don't understand you, Mother," says Raven. "If you don't like us, why did you save our lives from the wave of lava?"

The Evil Queen sighs. "That was my 'hexplaining obvious things is hexhausting' sigh, if you didn't pick up on that. I didn't save *all* your lives, daughter. I was just trying to save—never mind."

"How many different kinds of sighs do you think she has?" whispers Maddie. "I'm guessing twenty-three."

"I'm fine walking in front by myself," Frankie offers with forced cheeriness.

"Breathing is a sign of life!" says Raven. "Living things breathe, breathing things live! The sound of breathing should bring you joy, if you have any heart at all!"

"You bring up an interesting point, my little grump-toad." The Evil Queen gestures to Frankie and Draculaura. "Why are *they* breathing at all?"

"Um," Frankie mutters, "I'm alive. Experts agree. I've heard it said. 'She's . . . *she's alive!*' Like that."

The Evil Queen gestures to Draculaura. "This, over here, is a vampire," she says, sounding like she's lecturing a small child. "And this, over here, is a zombie."

Frankie whirls to look behind her, worried one of the Zomboyz is tagging along.

"She means you," Apple whispers, stepping up beside her.

"But I'm not a zombie," Frankie says.

Apple shrugs. "The Evil Queen says weird stuff sometimes. She called me an Ambling McIntosh once."

"What does that even mean?"

"No idea," Apple says. "She's called me lots of names. There was also Fruitspawn," Apple continues, counting on her fingers, "Little Miss Undertow, Moldy Sock Puppet, Snowflake, and Fate's Toadie."

Frankie laughs, then covers her mouth. "Sorry. I'm not laughing at you. It's just...those names are nuts."

"They are," Apple agrees. "I want to laugh each time, but I'm always too scared of being roasted alive or turned into a frog or something."

"I don't get it. If she's trying to insult you, wouldn't she want to say something that makes sense?"

"I don't know," Apple says. "But the *way* people say something means something."

"You're right," Frankie says. "It almost doesn't matter what the words are; if they say it like they, I don't know, think they're better than you? Or it makes you feel like you're worth less than they are? And that they're disgusted you even exist? It's not hate, exactly, but—"

"Contempt," Apple says. "Insults hurt, but so does saying things that *should* be nice but in a way that sounds scornful. Like 'your hair looks...fableous?'"

The way Apple pauses before *fableous* and implies a question at the end makes Frankie brush her fingers through her own black-and-white hair just to make sure it's okay.

"Or calling someone *princess*," Frankie says. She had been using that word from the first time she met Apple, and not in a particularly nice way. At first Frankie thought it was a kind of joke, because who really claims to be a princess? She felt out of place, and Draculaura was getting along so well with Raven, and here was Apple, this perfect girl who was also a princess and clearly thought monsters were terrible. So Frankie crammed all her "you think you're so special; you're not better than me; you're just a faker" feelings into the way she said that word. *Princess.* Now electricity surges through Frankie, turning her mint-green cheeks a pale pink.

"Or *monster*," Apple says. "The way I've been saying that word to you is... wrong."

"I'm sorry," they both say at the same time.

Apple pulls Frankie into a hug that almost pops a seam at her shoulder.

"Do you smell that?" Frankie asks.

Apple releases her. "It wasn't me."

"No, not that," Frankie says, looking around. "And not *smell*, exactly…"

"Just *stop it*, already!" Raven is yelling, still arguing with her mother.

"I'm just saying you shouldn't hang out with them too long," the Evil Queen says. "They're bound to eat you, steal your shoes, drink your blood, whatever. It's in their nature."

"That's a common misconception, actually—" Draculaura begins.

"*They are nice!*" Raven shouts. "*And they are my friends!*"

Frankie's eyes widen as she realizes what she smells. Or *senses*. There is lightning nearby, and a lot of it. Until now, there's been no weather of any kind in the Margins, but her ears are good at picking up the crackle of electricity. It's almost like electricity whispers to her: *Hey, Frankie, just hanging out inside the wires in the walls, no worries*, or *Having a keen time circling inside this battery—wheee!* or *Right above you, girl! I'm tired of this cloud, and I'm coming down!*

She was hearing it now, except instead of polite

conversation, the lightning was shouting like two armies on either side of the bridge. *AARRGGHHH!*

"Look out!" shouts Frankie. She shoves Raven and the Evil Queen away just as imaginary lightning crackles out of imaginary clouds, zapping Frankie in a way that doesn't feel imaginary at all. Her bolts buzz; her hair lifts. She smiles and can feel her teeth shudder. Refreshing, actually.

"Whoa," says Raven. "Thanks, Frankie."

"Okay, Sparky and Sparky Junior," Maddie says, cartwheeling between Raven and her mother. "Let's separate you two."

"Great idea, Maddie," Apple says, eyeing the clouds. "How about Frankie, Raven, and I take the front, and you, Draculaura, and, er, Her Highness guard the rear."

The two Queens scowl at each other over Maddie's head.

"Cool!" Draculaura chirps. "I'll tell you all about vampires! My dad is thousands of years old, you know?"

The Evil Queen drops her glare. "Is that possible?"

"Totes!" Draculaura says.

"Hexplain, vampire girl."

"Whew." Apple exhales as she, Frankie, and Raven pull ahead.

The clouds stop sparking and fade into dark wisps of fog.

"That was the Margins, I guess," Frankie says. "Forming your anger into a storm."

"Sorry," Raven says. "She just makes me so mad. And I felt like I could cut loose because, you know, here there's no risk of it turning into a magical fight."

"Hexcept for the imaginary doom clouds," says Apple.

"As if we needed more natural disaster," says Frankie. "What with the entire world breaking into pieces and all."

She picks a screw out of her pocket and tosses it over the bridge. When they first left Ever After High, the lava was so far down she couldn't hear a splash. After they left the Lost Library, screws had taken four seconds to hit the lava. Now it took two.

"It's rising," Apple says.

"That's right," Frankie confirms.

Apple takes out the Mapalogue she confiscated

from the Evil Queen and has been carrying in her backpack.

"We better get to this Shadow High place fast," says Apple. "We're running out of time."

"Let's walk faster," says Raven, picking up the pace.

Frankie starts laughing.

"What?" asks Apple, smiling even though she doesn't yet know what's funny.

"We're in the Margins, ghouls!" says Frankie. "Why are we walking?"

She shuts her eyes and imagines so hard her lightning-recharged body fizzles all over. In the fog ahead, a train whistle sounds.

Along the bridge now lies a track, and a mint-green-and-silver engine waits, smoke billowing out of its steam stack. It makes an impatient *whoo-whoo* noise.

The group climbs into the single train car, and with some focused imagining from Frankie, the engine starts to pull them down the track. *Chk-chk-chk-chk*, faster and faster, the track lying before them as they steam ahead.

"Wahoo!" Raven yells, her head out the window.

MAPALOGUE

The Lost Library

Shadow High

Monster High

Normie High

Frankie laughs again.

There are no more forks in the bridge. The train carries them straight down the bridge toward an island obscured by the thick mist. Suddenly, the engine breaks through the fog and disappears. A second later, the train car vanishes, dumping them all on the end of the bridge.

Ahead, an island is adorned with the blackened towers of a once-great castle. Through the very center of the building, a volcano rises, its peak a hundred feet above the building's roof. From the mouth of the volcano, a slow flow of angry liquid fire trickles out, a line of bright gold running off the edge and into that ocean of Unmaking.

"Thanks for riding the *Stein Express*," Frankie says. "We have arrived at our final destination, Shadow High."

CHAPTER 24

FRANKIE SHIVERS WITH LOOSE ELECTRICITY BUT keeps her feet moving, one after the other. Dead ahead, Shadow High rises up through the mist. Black. As tall as a mountain. As scary as a fairytale come to life.[73]

The white stone bridge merges with the island's white stone foundation, the only substance that the Unmaking doesn't seem able to unmake. As Frankie steps through the damp fog and onto the island, the air changes. Dry as sunbaked bones, the air rattles in

---

[73] It turns out that, from a monster's point of view, living fairytales are pretty frightening.

her lungs and makes her fingertips feel like paper. Tiny letters move around in a breeze:

AIR, AIR, AIR...

The group walks to the front of the ancient school and stands there, staring up.

From a distance, the school appeared to be formed from twisted and blackened iron, but as Frankie squints at it, she can make out letters, huge letters running up and down its length: S H A D O W H I G H, S H A D O W H I G H...Peering closer, she sees that the big words are formed from smaller words: W A L L, W I N D O W, D O O R, S T E P...The ground is littered with F L O W E R, P E B B L E, P E B B L E, P E B B L E, L O S T B A C K P A C K, S N O T T Y T I S S U E, W A D O F G U M...

Like the Lost Library, this school was unmade, the lava taking away its substance and leaving just the words. But this building was unmade so long ago the letters left behind are covered with some kind of hard black growth, like an anchor that was abandoned at the bottom of the ocean.

The source of the Unmaking is clear: the huge black volcano sprouting right up through the center of the building, the roof broken into a gaping hole around it.

Frankie sighs. This place is *almost* really cool. If only there were a full moon shining silver against the wall of fog, a sizzling lightning storm and the comforting rumble of thunder, a nice respectable cemetery around the school, maybe a few howling werewolves and a shambling zombie or two. But this place isn't monster-scary. It is empty-scary, eerie-scary. The wrongness of it gives Frankie such a bad case of goosebumps that her shivering is getting out of control. Her neck bolts buzz and splutter, and all she wants is to run straight home to the old laboratory and curl up on a metal slab.

But she can't let herself run away. She stares up at the school with the others and sighs again.

"*Whoa*," says Raven.

"*Ugh*," says Apple.

"*Creee*-py," says Draculaura.

"*Well, well, well*," says the Evil Queen.

"*Pupstutterbug*," says Maddie.

Frankie doesn't even bother to ask what *pupstutterbug* means. At this point, she knows Maddie would just answer with something like "Pupstutterbug is when a thing doesn't sing but it should. You know, like beetles!"

Frankie scowls. If she hadn't tried to be so amazing with her report and make the Mapalogue do things it wasn't supposed to do, they wouldn't be in this mess. So she is the first up the S T E P, S T E P, S T E P, S T E P and to the F R O N T D O O R. She puts her hand on the K N O B and turns. The delicate lacework of *D*s and *O*s and *R*s slowly swings open on H I N G E S, creaking but staying intact. She takes a step onto the F L O O R. The tips of the *F*s, *L*s, *O*s, and *R*s chip off and crunch beneath her boot, leaving a fine black dust.

"*Hellooooo?*" she calls out. "Anybody home?"

The Evil Queen mutters,

Find, seek, identify the weak and hidden, make them come bidden.

She shakes her hands out. A tiny fizzle of orange magic sparks from her fingertips before sputtering into nothing with a sound like a sad little blow of a kazoo.

"Impossible!" she says.

"My magic didn't work in the Margins, but it did work on the Lost Library island," Raven says. "I thought it would work here, too. Is this place dampening magic?" She tries the spell. Her fizzle and splutter are even smaller.

"Aw," says Maddie. "Your magic spells are all tuckered out, poor things."

"This place was supposed to have *more* power." The Evil Queen tilts her face up and yells, "What a wretched hexcuse for a secret site of unfathomable power you are, Shadow High!"

"Wahoo!" cheers Apple, startling Frankie.

Frankie frowns at her, even more goosebumps prickling her skin. Basically, her goosebumps have goosebumps. "What?"

"I mean," says Apple, shrugging, "we made it. We're here. Now we can save the world and all that. I know it's fairy creepy, but, well, if Briar were here, she would spellebrate that we made it, at least."

"Wahoo," Frankie whispers. That instinct to run away is like lightning rushing through her limbs. She tries to turn on the compass, but though it spins, the magic part of it fizzles out, too.

"No arrow pointy thingy," says Draculaura.

"Oh curses." Raven takes the chisel out of the compass and peeks into the first CLASSROOM. "So, where are we supposed to put the chisel?"

Fact: The chisel's slot is in the mouth of the volcano, says a voice.

Apple jumps back so fast her tiara falls over her eyes. She's staring at something Frankie can't see, and her knees are visibly shaking.

"Who—who are you?" Apple asks.

Declarative statement: I am Ms. Direction, says the voice.

Draculaura pops into bat form, apparently without meaning to. She flaps around, muttering, "I have a bad, bad feeling! A bad, bad feeling!"

Frankie can *hear* Ms. Direction's voice, and yet she can't describe what it sounds like. Not high or low, not soft or strong, no accent or personality to the voice at all. It's as though the words just slide right through her ears and into her mind. The effect is so odd she feels funny in her middle and checks the seam there for loose moths.

"Hiding is the first recourse of weasels!" the Evil Queen says, looking around. "I demand you reveal yourself to me! Your secrets shall be my treasures!"

Definition: A treasure (noun) is something precious. Secrets are not precious to you, Evil Queen. Power is precious. And here you have none. Do not command Ms. Direction.

The Evil Queen blinks. Her mouth closes.

"Mom?" says Raven, taking a step closer. "Are you okay?"[74]

"But *what* are you?" Apple asks, still staring straight ahead, her pale chin trembling.

Repetition: I am Ms. Direction, she says again. *Don't be afraid, Apple White.*

Immediately, Apple's chin stops quivering, her knees stop trembling. Her forehead wrinkles smooth, and she stands up straight, calm, almost uninterested.

Frankie approaches Apple. She's about to ask if Apple's okay, when suddenly, a woman appears in front of Apple. Frankie takes a step back, and the woman disappears. She nears Apple, and again the woman is visible. She is tall and thin, her hair up in a bun, and everything about her is colorless—skin, hair, clothes, all shades of gray, like watered-down ink.

---

74 I'm with Raven. The Evil Queen doesn't shut up just because someone told her to. Something is definitely wrong.

Frankie squints. The woman is made entirely of tiny words. HAIR, FOREHEAD, EYEBROW, NOSE...

"She's there!" says Frankie, pointing. "She's right there! But you can only see her from one point of view. Or she's like a page of a book, obvious from the front but thin as paper from the side."

Analysis: You are correct, Frankie Stein, announces Ms. Direction.

For some reason, Ms. Direction's words make Frankie feel amazing, as if her favorite teacher just put a shiny gold star on her forehead. She wants to do something else that will gain approval. A handstand, maybe? She could juggle. She looks around, can't see anything to juggle, and briefly considers loosening one of her hands and juggling it with the other.

Instead, she says, "You're Ms. Direction, so you made this school! My friend Draculaura and I kinda, sorta founded a school, too."

Correct, you and Draculaura founded the current Monster High. Exception: I am not the Ms. Direction who founded this school. She has been gone a long time. I am what is left of her.

"You are...her words," says the Evil Queen, slowly and through gritted teeth, as if it's hard for her to speak. "You are her *power*."

"Ghouls, we should get going," says Bat-Drac.

"Right, let's climb that volcano," says Raven.

Directive: Draculaura flies up high into the air. Then she falls.

Bat-Drac spirals up to the CEILING and then her wings just stop. She falls like a stone.

"Drac!" yells Frankie, running to catch her friend.

Raven reaches her first, and the bat lands in Raven's hands with a little *plop*. Raven cradles her in her palms. "Are you okay? What happened?"

"I don't know," says Draculaura. "I had to do what she said."

"What are you doing?" Frankie shouts out to Ms. Direction. "What do you want?"

Fact: Stories are flawed. It is impossible to narrate a flawless story when the characters do whatever they want.

"Welp, I do six impossible things before breakfast," says Maddie.

Too much uncertainty in stories. Too many errors. Characters resist being controlled and do things that ruin the plot. Confession: I found the power to break a story down to its raw pieces so I could rebuild them the way I wanted. Result: It worked, at first. But the power . . . was too great.

"The Unmaking lava started to flow freely," says Raven. "And instead of making it easier to control the stories, it just took everything apart."

For thousands of years I have been alone on this island. I know all the stories happening out there, but I cannot control them. It must stop. You must stop. It is time.

"Ms. Direction, you can help us finish this story!" says Frankie.

No. You will stop. Sit down, Frankie Stein.

Frankie sits on the R U G, R U G, R U G. "I don't want to sit down," she says. But she can't stand up. It's not that the body her father made her has stopped working. It's as if her thoughts are separate from her body. She can think but she can't do.

No more talking, Frankie Stein. Sit down, girls. Everyone sits down. No dialogue and no action means no story. No more story.

Bat-Drac is still curled up in Raven's hand. Raven and Apple sit down beside the Evil Queen. But Maddie . . .

"Are we playing a game?" asks Maddie. She starts

to circle the group, touching their heads and saying, "Duck, duck, duck, *notaduck*!"

Explanation: Ms. Direction said everyone sits down.

"I'm not an everyone," says Maddie. "Duck, duck…"

Madeline Hatter stops moving.

Maddie blows air out of her lips. "Stop moving? I don't even know what that means! I never stop."

Madeline Hatter sits down.

Maddie cartwheels. "Why is everyone being so silly? We're in spooky Shadow High! We should tell ghost stories and play goblin-in-the-dark."

Madeline Hatter has a tea party.

"Now you're making sense!" Maddie rummages around in her hat. "I'm sure I have a tea party in here somewhere…." Maddie sits on the floor and pulls out a teacup. It's empty, but she pretends to drink from it.

Madeline Hatter has a tea party forever.

What? No! You can't do that! I am Brooke Page, the Narrator of this story, and I'm telling you to stop it, Ms. Direction. You are breaking all the rules. And besides that, it's just mean to make characters do what they wouldn't normally do. Mean and not nice and…and not at all professional!

The Evil Queen joins Maddie's tea party. She sits on the floor. Forever.

Oh yeah? Well, the Evil Queen doesn't sit on the floor. The Evil Queen gets her magic back and… and she puts a spell on Ms. Direction that makes Ms. Direction be quiet and never talk again!

The Evil Queen is happy to sit down and be still. She wonders why she ever desired power in the first place. Now all she wants to do is have a tea party.[75]

This is bad. This is really bad. Move, girls! Don't listen to Ms. Direction. Get up that volcano, put the chisel back, save the world! Move!

The characters do not move, says Ms. Direction. *The characters wait. They wait for it all to be over. They do nothing as they wait for The End.*

Unfortunately, The End may be closer than any of them want. Frankie can't stand and she can't speak, but she can see. Through the spaces between the letters W I N D O W, Frankie can see outside the

---

75 Reader, the Evil Queen is just sitting there, smiling and clinking teacups with Maddie. My commands aren't strong enough to overcome Ms. Direction's commands. Oh *italics*, what should I do?

school. There are large shapes in the fog, moving closer. The islands of the other lands are arriving at Shadow High. The spaces between them are narrow, the Unmaking lava rising up, just inches below the shoreline. The air is golden with the lava's light.

CHAPTER 25

MOM! DAD!

Brookey, I'm sorry. I'm so sorry this is happening.

We feared from the beginning that this would be The End. We only wanted to spare you from watching it all coming.

There has to be some way we can help! The girls have come so far. They've done all they can do. It's not fair!

Stories aren't always fair to their characters. Sometimes talking spiders die. Sometimes little boys get sick and their stuffed bunnies get thrown away. Sometimes bad things happen to characters.

But...but there's got to be something! Mom, can't you narrate the characters free? Dad, can't you change the story?

Narrators don't have that kind of power, Brooke. Ms. Direction got that power for herself, but with it came the Unmaking.

If we tried to narrate the story to make it do what we wanted, that volcano could erupt again, bringing The End even faster.

We can only narrate what the characters do.

I wish I were a character in the story, and then I'd do something. Me and Frankie and Raven together. And...and if we were in the Margins, we could imagine everyone away from Ms. Direction. Wait...there was something I read about imagination in school. The entire World of Stories exists because the Readers have incredible imaginations. Right?

The job of Narrators is quite small, really. Though we put the words to the story, it's the Readers who do most of the work by making the story come alive in their minds.

So, Mom, you'd say that the Readers are powerful? Even more powerful than Ms. Direction?

Wait, I know what you have in mind, Brooke.

Please, Dad?

That is a very dangerous idea, young lady.

Please? I need to enter the story. I need to be a character. So that means I need a Narrator to narrate me.

I'm worried about our baby girl.

Me too. But she's the best chance these worlds have.

CHAPTER 26

In the Land of Narrators, Brooke Page is running.

She is running past her house, down the street, through town. Narrators line the block to watch her, their mouths open, because they've never seen a Narrator become a character in a story before.

"You can do it, Brooke!" someone yells.

A few applaud. The applause grows louder and louder, and it feels like approving pats on her back.

Brooke smiles. She believes she can. Her parents hope she can. And though they are very, very, very, very, very worried, they are still narrating her. They are narrating her at this very second because they believe she can do it, too.

At the edge of town, Brooke enters the Grammar Forest, hopping over root words and ducking under the dangling participles. A breeze weaves through the trees, pushing fallen nouns into piles on the ground. Verbs hop, wiggle, and march by, and Brooke leaps over them. Adjectives float like seed puffs, sticking to anything they touch. She brushes several adjectives out of her hair and runs faster.

At last, coming out from under the foreshadows of the forest canopy, Brooke sees it. The Fourth Wall. The great wall runs the stacks' length of the World of Stories, creating a barrier between this world and the Readers' World. It is white, like the stone land under Shadow High, like the bridges in the Margins, a foundation that is and always will be.

Brooke climbs the Fourth Wall.

The wall is uneven, and there are places to grab with her fingers and tiny holes for her toes.

Soon she is high, much, much higher than her mother would like. So high that her father's heart is pounding hard with worry, and he's sweating like a buffalo.

And then her foot slips.

No, Brooke! Be careful! If she falls, it's a long way down.

Brooke spots some adjectives still stuck to her from her run through the Grammar Forest. She peels the word *sticky* off her arm and places it on the bottom of her shoe. Now her shoe sticks to the wall. It's the extra lift she needs.

She pulls herself to the top of the wall and looks over.

The land of Readers! Mostly she can see only fog over the world—thick, white, seemingly solid, like the kind that fills the Margins.

"Of course," she says. "Just like in the Margins, magic spells don't work in the Readers' World, but imagination is extra powerful."

She stands up on the narrow top of the Fourth Wall. Through the fog she thinks she can see buildings, streets, houses. And when she squints, she sees people. Busy. Everyone so busy, moving and living and working and studying and just being. It's the land of Readers, and yet not many of them are reading, not right at this moment, when she so desperately needs them. She hopes there is at least one. One with a book open, ready for a story.

Brooke clears her throat.

"*Ahem.* Halloo! Hey, uh, Reader! I need you. We need you. Raven, Apple, Frankie, Drac, and Maddie need you. Even the Evil Queen needs you! They're stuck. It's not supposed to go like this. Ms. Direction is cheating, you see. She broke the rules. She's trying to bring on The End before the heroes have a chance to finish the story. Can you help?"

Brooke listens. No response.

"I said, *can you help?*"

Reader, answer her! Yes, *you.* You are the Reader. Please say yes now so Brooke can hear you. She needs to know you're listening.

Please?

...

Through the fog, Brooke hears a faint *"YES!"*

"Yay!" says Brooke. "Thank you! I need you to help change the story. I don't know what will work. I just know that the heroes are stuck and they've done all they can. Can you do the rest? If you think up a way for them to escape Ms. Direction and imagine it, you're so powerful that you can actually make it happen. I have some ideas. Go to the next chapter if you're willing to try."

CHAPTER 27

O KAY. THERE MUST BE SOME WAY OUR HEROES can overcome Ms. Direction, *if she weren't cheating like a big meanie*! Reader, I'm going to give you some options, and you choose what you think should happen next in the story.

Who do you think will be the key to over-coming Ms. Direction?

If Raven is the key, go to page 272.
If Frankie is the key, go to page 273.
If Maddie is the key, go to page 274.

Ms. Direction told Raven to sit down but not to be quiet. That means Raven can still speak!

If Raven asks her mom for help, go to page 275.
If Raven asks Draculaura for help, go to page 276.

Frankie can't get up off the floor. She can't speak. But her right hand is loose. She wiggles it, and the hand comes free.

If Frankie sends her hand over to Apple, go to page 277.
If Frankie sends her hand around the school, go to page 278.

Maddie can speak. She can move. But Ms. Direction commanded her to have a tea party forever. Maddie is having a horriblicious, baffle-worthy idea: A forever tea party might *not* be as splendiful as it sounds, not when Unmaking is bubbling up out of the trenches between lands. Not when her friends look as sad as a sandwich left out in the rain. And certainly *not* when the Evil Queen keeps hogging all the pretend tea cakes!

If Maddie invites Ms. Direction to join the tea party, go to page 279.
If Maddie tries to narrate the story herself, go to page 281.

"Mom," Raven whispers. "Our magic is dampened here but not gone. Grab my hand so we can combine our power. Let's try Arabeth's Spell of Silence?"

If the Evil Queen nods in agreement, go to page 283.
If the Evil Queen turns away, go to page 284.

Draculaura is curled up in Raven's hand, her small, leathery wings wrapped around her body like blankets.

"Drac," Raven whispers, "she commanded us all to sit down, but you're not sitting. You're a bat—you can't sit down. Blink if you think you can move."

Bat-Drac blinks her small black eyes.

If Raven tells Draculaura to use her bat sonic squeals on Ms. Direction, go to page 285. If Raven gives Draculaura the chisel to fly up to the volcano, go to page 286.

Frankie's green hand taps Apple's white one. Apple startles, glances at Ms. Direction, and quickly composes herself. She looks back at the rest of Frankie and makes a "what now?" expression.

If Frankie mimes singing, go to page 287.
If Frankie's hand gestures toward the chisel, go to page 289.

Frankie's hand runs behind Ms. Direction and begins to explore the school. Everywhere, everything is made up of letters. Frankie's fingers start to pick letters from their word chains and build new words.

If Frankie's hand builds the word *wire*, go to page 290.
If Frankie's hand builds the words *wide hole*, go to page 292.

"Wow, this is the *best tea party ever*," says Maddie, smiling extra huge. "Isn't it, Evily Queenie?"

The Evil Queen can't speak, but she nods, her eyes wide as she sips nothing from her teacup.

"Why, I haven't had *this much fun* since we played cupcake croquet in the Castleteria. Ms. Direction, come and join us!"

Query: Madeline Hatter invites me to a tea party? asks Ms. Direction.

"Oh yes, come and sit and have tea and cakes. Now, tell us about your day, your favorite colors, and if you had the choice, whether you'd prefer to have an elephant trunk or a spider monkey tail."

Ms. Direction looks down at her HANDS.

Confession: The Ms. Direction who was, long ago, would have loved to have a tea party with Madeline Hatter.

She plops down on the F L O O R and her
M O U T H changes into a S M I L E.

"Move down, move down, make room for
Ms. Direction!" says Maddie.

The Evil Queen hands the ancient Narrator
a teacup. And suddenly, everybody can move
freely.

Go to page 294.

" 'Then I'll do it myself,' Maddie says."

Question: Pardon? asks Ms. Direction.

"Oh, right!" says Maddie. "Um…open quote then I'll do it myself comma close quote Maddie says."

Follow-up question: Is Madeline Hatter attempting to narrate?

"Madeline Hatter, known by her friends as Maddie, and by some mice as 'the great furless giant,' finishes her tea party."

Statement: This will not do, says Ms. Direction. *The tea party goes on forever.*

"Maddie giggles. 'Tea parties are parties; they are not forevers,' she says."

Assertion: This is impossible. You are not the Narrator. You are a character. The Narrator cannot be a character. A character cannot be the Narrator.

"Maddie laughs because Maddie has been both a character *and* a Narrator before, so this is the possible kind of impossible. 'Ms. Direction?' Maddie asks. 'Are you the Narrator of this story or a character in it?'"

Paradox: Ms. Direction is…I…am neither. I am both?

"And so then Ms. Direction got so confused that her letters got all scrambly and her powers got all scampery and nobody had to do what she said anymore," Maddie narrates.

Go to page 294.

With an effort that brings beads of sweat to her forehead, the Evil Queen puts down her teacup and reaches out. Raven puts Bat-Drac in her lap and takes her mother's hand. Her heart beats hard and fast, and she feels so much love for her strange, evil mother right now it's like her chest is a whole warm pumpkin pie. Together, they speak aloud the words of the spell:

> A cloak, a shell, a silence spell.
> Take her sound beyond, below,
> and in an eternal casket stow.

What are you do— Ms. Direction starts to say. But it's too late. With their combined power, they managed to finish the casting. Ms. Direction is enspelled in silence forevermore.

Go to page 294.

Raven's face turns red with anger. Even here, even now, her mother won't help her! She speaks the spell by herself.

"A cloak, a shell, a silence spell…" It's a simple spell that requires little magic, but the faint amount she summons up in this place isn't enough. The enchantment of silence fizzles out of her fingers, falling like dust on the F L O O R.

Raven Queen, give up, speak not more, be silent, says Ms. Direction.

Raven has no choice but to obey.

This path has failed. Return to page 271.

Bat-Drac flaps into the air with a sudden flurry of black wings and dives at Ms. Direction, swooping at her face and straight through her insubstantial HEAD.

Draculaura opens her tiny, toothy mouth and emits a sonic scream. The microscopic letters that make up Ms. Direction's head vibrate.

Draculaura will... Draculaura will... Ms. Direction tries to speak, but Draculaura keeps screeching, and the letters that are all that's left of the ancient Narrator keep vibrating—until they collapse into a heap on the floor.

Go to page 294.

Draculaura flaps her wings and perches on Raven's hand. She grips the chisel in her tiny black claws and takes flight. Immediately, the weight of the chisel pulls her down. Draculaura scrambles to get airborne.

Ms. Direction's blinkless EYES turn on her.

Command: Draculaura drops the chisel. Draculaura does not move. Raven picks up the chisel.

No, Raven thinks as she picks up the chisel, her icy stomach anticipating what Ms. Direction will say next. *Don't, don't —*

Raven throws the chisel into the lava, narrates Ms. Direction.

Raven stumbles out of the school and to the end of the island. The lava is so high now it bubbles just over the edge. She wants to cry when her hand tosses the chisel into the lava, where the letters CHISEL slowly sink beneath the surface.

This path has failed. Return to page 271.

Apple nods. She doesn't look so sure, but she starts to sing a happy little tune.

"*Tra-la-la and fiddledeedee, whatever will become of me?*" sings Apple.

Question: What is Apple White doing?

"*By Miss Muffet's whey and curds, if only I could find some birds,*" sings Apple.

Nothing lives on Shadow High's island, and yet the echoes of the creatures who once inhabited the place hear Apple White. In through the W I N D O W come jumbles of letters in intricate patterns. As they flap past Frankie, she sees that they are made up of *B*s, *I*s, *R*s, and *D*s.

The B I R D S circle Apple White, and then they fly at Ms. Direction, sharp B E A K S forward. They rustle the ancient Narrator's letters. She bats at them with her H A N D S. But then—

Apple White starts to sneeze, says Ms. Direction. *She sneezes so hard she can no longer sing.*

"*Little birdies come*—choo! Achool *Come here and*—ACHOO!"

It is impossible to stop Ms. Direction, says Ms. Direction. And it would seem that she is right.

This path has failed. Return to page 271.

Apple smiles and flips her hair. There's so much of that glorious blond hair it shields the movement of her hand as she grabs the chisel from Raven and sticks it behind her back.

Frankie's hand takes it from Apple with two fingers and crawls with the other three. The volcano is within sight but seems to be a world away.

Observation: Frankie Stein is a clever girl. But her hand is crawling the wrong way. Her hand will instead throw the chisel off the edge of the island and into the Unmaking lava.

Unfortunately, even Frankie's severed hand obeys Ms. Direction.

This path has failed. Return to page 271.

Frankie's hand drags back a long, thin line made up of letters it has pieced together: W I R E, W I R E, W I R E...

Apple spies what Frankie is up to, looks at Ms. Direction, and starts to sing loudly and distractingly.

"Hey diddle diddle, the cat asks a riddle, the cow eats a prune with a spoon!"

What is Apple White doing? asks Ms. Direction, looking at Apple and not Frankie's hand.

Frankie's hand attaches the W I R E to one of her neck bolts, runs it over to Ms. Direction, and wraps it around her ANKLE.

Apple White stops singing, says Ms. Direction.

Frankie takes a deep breath, and all that tingly, warm electricity gathers in her middle. She sends it shooting to her neck bolt, where it travels along the W I R E. The electric current rattles all the tiny letters that make up Ms. Direction. They shift and tremble, pop like popcorn, and then fall into a harmless heap.

Go to page 294.

Frankie's hand scampers back with a string of letters pieced together: W I D E H O L E. She holds the O on her pinkie, careful not to insert it until the words are spread beneath the feet of Ms. Direction.

What is young Frankie Stein doing? asks Ms. Direction just as Frankie's hand inserts the O into the newly formed W I D E H O L E.

Ms. Direction falls into the hole. But before she's completely gone, she catches the lip of the words and plucks out three of the letters: I D E. Instantly, the hole vanishes, leaving Ms. Direction's upper half sitting on the floor, the rest of her still swallowed up in the floor.

Frankie hoped Ms. Direction would fall entirely into the hole, but perhaps her efforts were good enough. Frankie tries to stand up. But her body still won't obey her.

Ms. Direction taps the remaining letters

around her into W H O L E and swallows them. Her body becomes whole again.

   Statement: You cannot best Ms. Direction in a contest of words.

This path has failed. Return to page 271.

You found a path that worked. But it's not quite enough. Sometimes to be really, really powerful, the imagination needs a nice blank page. Here is some space for you to think through what way our heroes overcome Ms. Direction. You can take an idea from the previous pages or make up your own entirely. And you can simply imagine it in your head or write it all down. (If this book doesn't belong to you, don't write in it, of course! Go ahead and write on a separate piece of paper and then stick it in the book to complete the magic.)

So here's the part where the story got stuck:

Ms. Direction has just commanded Frankie, Apple, and Raven to sit down on the F L O O R *of Shadow High. Bat-Drac is curled up in Raven's hand. Maddie and the Evil Queen are locked in an eternal tea party. No one seems able to resist Ms. Direction's power and stand up. All seems lost.*

They need you! Write or imagine what the characters do to get free of Ms. Direction so they can head toward the volcano:

Hooray! You did it, Reader! Thank you! Now I can get back to narrating the story.

Freed from Ms. Direction's power, the girls and the Evil Queen rush through the S C H O O L and to the volcano's steep slope. Raven is the first to start the climb, with Bat-Drac fluttering at her shoulder.

CHAPTER 28

RAVEN PANTS AS SHE RUNS UP THE VOLCANO. The slope is so steep she has to use her hands as well as her feet, crawl-running and feeling like a mountain goat. The volcano itself is black as ink and made up of solid letters—V O L C A N O, V O L C A N O, V O L C A N O—melted together into a rough, thick crust.

By the time she's close to the top, she's slowed from a goat-crawl to a snail-crawl, her breath stinging in her throat. Climbing a treacherous volcano while scared for her life turns out to be more difficult than she imagined. She stops at the crest, gasping for breath. Just over the lip bubbles a pool of bright-as-sunlight Unmaking lava.

Draculaura in bat form lands next to her.

"I can see it," she squeaks, popping back into human form. Immediately, a R O C K gives way under her feet, and she starts to slip. Raven's heart jumps as Draculaura tips toward the opening and the lava below, but she turns back into a bat.

"I guess I'll keep my wings," she says, eyeing the lava nervously. "I don't know how you were able to get up here without falling. Climbing in heels is scary-hard."

"Climbing in one shoe isn't a picnic." Apple takes off her remaining shoe and tosses it away.

"Try climbing…in heels…*and* a cape," the Evil Queen says, panting, from the rear of the group.

"What did you see, Drac?" Raven asks.

"In the center of the lava pool," Draculaura says, pointing with a wing, "there's a flat white rock. The lava flows around it, and in the middle of the rock there's a smallish hole."

Raven peers over the edge. This close to the lava, she feels a strange heat, and her face prickles, but not from sweat. The very outer layer of her skin is turning into microscopic letters, each dust-size *S*, *K*, *I*, and *N* flaking off and floating away.

The lake of lava is dotted with half a dozen out-croppings of white rock, most barely big enough to stand on. But in the center Raven sees the one Draculaura is talking about. And while bigger than the others, it is not so big you'd feel comfortable jumping on it in the middle of a lava lake.

"I could fly it over, maybe," Bat-Drac squeaks.

Draculaura is big for a bat, but the chisel is more than half her size.

The others reach the top of the volcano.

"Whoa," Frankie says, peering in.

"That…does not seem safe," Apple says.

"The bat should fly the chisel in," says the Evil Queen.

"There's no way she could carry it, Mother," says Raven.

"I have a black ribbon from my headdress I'm willing to sacrifice," the Evil Queen says. "Just tie the chisel to the bat's body."

Draculaura twitches. "I…er…guess we could *try* that."

"No," says Raven.

"Then send the walking abomination," says the Evil Queen.

Everyone stares at the queen.

"The...*Frankie*," she amends. "If Frankie falls in and loses an arm or leg, we just get her another one, stitch it on, no loss."

Frankie hugs herself, and Apple puts a protective hand on her shoulder.

"I'll do this," Raven says. "This whole thing is your—is our family's fault. We have to fix it."

"Well, if my magic were working properly, certainly," says the Evil Queen. "But I am not equipped for walking on lava, so one of them will have to use their dubious skills."

"*I can see my house from here!*" Maddie shouts.

Raven snorts a surprised laugh. But then it turns out Maddie *can* see her house from there. They all can. The Margins are narrowing, and the fog is thinning. From high atop the volcano, they have a view of Book End, the village that has been Maddie and her father's home since they left Wonderland. On a separate island approaches the unmistakable outline of Ever After High.

"Oh no," Draculaura says.

On the opposite shore of the volcano, another shape, another island creeps nearer: a forested hill, and on it the terraces and spires of a school.

"Monster High," Frankie says.

From every side they come, individual lands, pulled irresistibly closer to Shadow High, all the lands of the World of Stories coming back together. Lands of forest, lands of deserts, lands entirely underwater. Houses and villages, farms and cities, and schools.

More schools! One resembles an ancient temple, built of white marble with tall pillars atop a huge and craggy mountain, lightning flashing at its peak. Another is candy-colored and bright, surrounded by a snowy landscape, and in the sky above it soars a kind of open carriage pulled by eight flying moose— or something moose-like. The girl seated inside it is dressed in a white-trimmed red suit and shouts, "Ho-ho-ho!"

"Oh curses, did you hear that evil laugh?" Apple says. "It came from those flying moose. Or mooses. Is it moose or mooses? Meese?"

"Please," scoffs the Evil Queen. "'Ho-ho-ho' hardly qualifies as an *evil* laugh."

"That sounded like Santa," Frankie says. "'Ho-ho-ho' is kind of his catchphrase."

"What is a Santa?" Raven asks.

"Santa Claus. Guy with a beard who rides around in a sleigh pulled by reindeer," Draculaura says. "Gives out presents."

"He sounds fairy nice," Apple says.

"But those particular 'ho-ho-hos' didn't sound like a man's," says Drac. "They sounded like a girl's."[76]

Raven forces her attention away from all the new lands and looks down. With the trenches between the lands so narrow, the Unmaking lava rises up, lapping like surf on their shores. There are *hundreds* of islands, places she had never imagined, places behind places, all closing in. And the closer those places get to Shadow High, the higher the lava climbs.

"Oh nose! I loved that bridge," Maddie says. The lava has crept over the edge of the Book End island and completely disassembled a BRIDGE on its shore.

Raven needs to act now or everything she's ever loved, everything anyone has ever loved, is going to

---

76 I've heard rumors that Santa Claus has a daughter! I wonder if it was her.

be destroyed. She stands, teetering on the edge of the volcano, and concentrates.

I fight for flight
that all might not fall
to endless night.

Eyes closed despite the risk of falling, Raven repeats the words until, in sputtering bursts, she feels the tingle of magic around her body, and her feet leave the ground. It's not full power, but perhaps the nearness of Ever After is boosting her magic a bit. She begins to rise.

"Foolish girl!" her mother exclaims.

Raven opens her eyes and focuses on the flat rock that holds the chisel's resting place. She glides slowly, several feet over the surface. A bubble rises in the lava. It is nothing to be concerned about, she tells herself. There are bubbles everywhere, and she only needs to focus on floating to her destination. The bubble pops, splashing Unmaking on the HEEL of her SHOE.

"*Aah*," Raven says, dipping lower in panic.

"Careful, Raven!" shouts Apple.

The tingle of M A G I C surrounding her wavers, the heat from the Unmaking unmaking it. She dips lower, and, desperate, she throws the chisel high and hard toward the white rock, hoping against hope that it will land magically in the socket before the lava swallows her.

Bat-Drac is there, clinging to the back of Raven's shirt with her claws and flapping like mad. The little bit of lift is just enough to help Raven land on one of the smaller rocks dotting the lake. What remains of Raven's shoes, jutting over the edge into the lava, sizzles into words, and then letters, and then ash.

Barefoot, Raven scrambles higher onto the rock as she watches the chisel arc above her and fall, clearly destined to splash several feet shy of the rock. It will land in the Unmaking, she knows, and everything will be lost. And it will all be her fault.

But a large green spider streaks out, grabbing the chisel in midair. Both chisel and spider tumble to a landing on the rock. The spider relinquishes its grip on the chisel and gives Raven a thumbs-up. Not a spider. Frankie's hand.

At the edge of the volcano, Frankie waves with a

handless arm. She had thrown her own hand and had caught the chisel.

"That was splendiferous!" says Maddie.

Frankie's hand grabs the chisel between middle and forefinger, pushing itself upright onto the three "legs" of pinkie, thumb, and ring finger. It waddles carefully to the socket and hooks the chisel into the edge. But the hand isn't tall enough to maneuver the chisel into the socket. It pushes and wiggles and tilts and inches but makes no progress.

"This is a job for Draculaura!" declares Bat-Drac. She leaves Raven and starts to fly to the chisel, but there is a sound of terrible grinding and thunder, and the volcano shakes.

BOOM! CRACK!

A large bubble of lava pops in front of her. She screeches and falls back. Raven grabs her out of the air. The little bat is dazed, eyes darting back and forth, wings all trembly. Raven tucks her safely inside her pocket.

"What's happening?" asks Raven.

"The islands are crashing into us!" Apple yells.

Frankie's hand struggles to stay upright, but the

weight of its burden overbalances it, and it stumbles. The chisel falls uselessly next to the socket, and the hand topples backward, over the edge of the stone, and right into the lava. The liquid swallows the hand, and a poof of smoke in the shape of H A N D floats into the air and vanishes.

"Bolts!" Frankie yells angrily from the shore.

"It's my fault!" Raven calls. "I can fix this!"

Raven closes her eyes and begins the spell again. *"I fight for flight…"*

"Don't, Raven!" the Evil Queen calls. "Narrator! Brooke!"

"That all might not fall…" Raven continues the spell.

"Brooke, what happened to the one who first put this chisel here?" her mother asks. "What happened to that Narrator?"

"…to endless night…"

Magic sparks fly erratically around Raven, and with jerks and sputters, she begins to rise.

"Where is he?" the Evil Queen shouts.

Raven hovers uneasily, dipping and tipping as she edges toward the spot where the chisel was first placed to save all the lands from destruction. The

Narrator who did that, no one knows his name, not anymore. He was never heard from again.

"Brooke says that Narrator was never heard from again!" says Maddie.

Raven glides over the lava and touches down on the white rock. She picks up the chisel.

"Raven, stop!" her mother yells. "Don't! It's a death sentence!"

Raven smiles at her mother. "I love you, Mother," she says. "Be good."

She moves to the socket, and in a flash of magical light the Evil Queen is there, pulling the chisel from her hand.

"Mother, what?" she manages to say before a wall of force erupts from her mother's palm, flinging Raven up and out of the lake. She arcs over the edge of the volcano and crashes into her friends, Frankie and Apple scrambling to catch her.

"What is she doing?" Frankie asks.

"She tricked us," Apple says. "She's—"

"Mother, *no*!" Raven shouts. "We have to return the chisel! There isn't any power here! Only destruction! There's no point!"

"Oh, daughter," the Evil Queen says, straightening her headdress. "You're only seeing part of the picture. If the chisel isn't returned, then destruction comes. Certainly. That's true."

"But—" Raven says.

"But this *is* power," the Evil Queen says, holding the chisel high. "More power than anyone before has ever possessed! I hold in my hands the power to destroy Ever After. And not just our home. *All* lands. Even the Narrators don't have that."

"*No!* We have the power to save them, Mother!"

The volcano groans as land grinds against land, and the lava creeps up their shores, taking apart G R A S S and F L O W E R S and T R E E S. On one land, as people flee, the first H O U S E loses itself to raw letters.

The Evil Queen holds up a finger. "*We* don't have the power to save them, dearie. *I* do. Would you have put the chisel in if I had not taken it?"

"Yes!"

"Of *course* you would have," the Evil Queen says. "Which means there was no other choice for you. You were trapped. Without choice, there is no power."

Raven closes her eyes and tries to say the spell,

tries to fly again, but her tongue feels heavy and the back of her head pulses with ache.

"Don't bother, my little Raven. It's not fair to leave a choice such as this to you. This is a mother's job, I think. So does the story of this world go on?" her mother asks, moving the chisel from one hand to the other. "Or does it jump forward to The End?"

She locks eyes with her daughter, and her face thaws into a smile that almost breaks Raven's heart.

"I prefer a world in which my daughter goes on," she says.

The Evil Queen eyes the socket and whispers something under her breath.[77] Then she jams in the chisel. There is a flash of blinding light and the sound of a thousand gongs banging at once. A hot wind shoves Raven. She glances back and sees the chisel in its socket, but her mother is just gone.

And then Raven whips through the air, rolls down the side of the volcano, and finally crashes in a painful heap at the bottom. Frankie is there; Maddie

---

77 Raven can't hear what her mother says, but I can, so here it is: "Reader! I thought the Narrators had all the power, but I was wrong. It's you. I know I'm the villain, but what's a story without a villain? I'm about to do something. Whether I survive is up to you. Personally, I think you should imagine that the Evil Queen can't die. Because that's what I think. And I'm usually right."

and Apple, too. Bat-Drac is starting to wake up in Raven's pocket.

A wind blows.

"Mom!" Raven yells, starting back up the volcano. The wind pushes at her, and she stumbles, unable to make any progress.

"They're moving apart," Apple shouts. "The lands are moving apart!"

All the islands that had drawn close are pushing back, separating from the land of Shadow High and one another. The lava between them lowers into the trenches. A wide bridge leads from Shadow High to Ever After High, but as the island recedes, the bridge grows thinner.

"We have to go!" Apple yells over the howling wind. "Now! If we want to get home at all, we need to go!"

Still staring up at the peak of the volcano, Raven allows Apple to pull her along.

"We can't follow you that way!" Frankie yells. "We have to go home."

She points in the opposite direction, to a different bridge, one that leads to Monster High.

Draculaura is back in her vampire form. Raven's

eyes are already wet. Draculaura pulls Raven into a strong vampire hug.

"This was so fun," she says, her voice cracking with emotion. "I'll never forget you, Raven Queen."

"I'll never forget you, Draculaura, the daughter of Dracula. And you, Frankie Stein, Frankenstein's daughter," Raven says, laughing a little through her tears. "You guys are going to have lots of adventures together."

"Wait, Maddie, what was our Narrator's name again?" asks Frankie.

"The tea-rrific, hat-tastic, splendiful Brooke!" says Maddie.

"Thank you, Brooke!" Frankie shouts.

"Yeah, you rock, Brooke!" says Raven.

"You're fairy, fairy brave," says Apple. "I'll always consider you a personal friend."

"Fangtastic, ghoul!" says Draculaura. "You saved the day, you know?"

"You saved the world," says Raven.[78]

"Time to go-oh, huggabugs!" Maddie calls. "Or

---

78 FYI, they said some other nice stuff, too, but I had to stop narrating to get a tissue. Happy tears are a thing.

we'll all have to live on this terrible hatless island forever!"

Frankie and Apple hug quickly.

"If anyone ever deserved the title of princess, it's you," Apple says.

Frankie smiles. "Keep the monster spirit alive. And don't let the haters get you down."

"Here," says Apple, tossing Frankie her backpack. "I got the Skullette from the Evil Queen when we were riding your amazing imaginary train. The Mapalogue is there, too!"

They give one another high fives, and then the girls run—Apple, Raven, and Maddie in one direction, Draculaura and Frankie in the other.

CHAPTER 29

THE BRIDGE STRETCHES LIKE BREAD DOUGH before them. The wind at her back makes Raven feel as if she can run faster than ever, but it still doesn't seem fast enough. The Village of Book End has reconnected with the Ever After High campus, but both are moving away as fast as the girls can run. And their bridge continues to thin.

"Single file!" Apple shouts, dropping behind Raven and Maddie.

The borders of the school are within sight, but Raven estimates they will be running on a bridge as narrow as thread in the next sixty seconds.

She knows she should imagine something to help them, but in her panic she can't think, she can't think....

"Faster!" Raven shouts.

"Did you cast a 'faster' spell on us?" Maddie calls from behind. "Points for quick casting, but I don't think it's working! I only feel as fast as regular Maddie!"

"Magic doesn't work in the Margins!" Raven yells back.

And then the bridge snaps.

Raven knows she should be scared, but more than anything, she is angry. Like waiting in line for an hour for an ice cream cone only to have the shop close right after the person in front of her. That kind of angry. The bridge was still a good ten inches wide when it snapped. It just wasn't fair.

And then Nevermore's giant clawed paw catches her midfall, another grabs Apple, and a toothy snout plucks Maddie from the air, holding her by the collar.

"Good girl!" Raven shouts.

"*Woo-hoo!*" Maddie howls, holding her arms wide.

The dragon flies through the fog of the Margins

toward the land of Ever After, rising higher and higher.

"Don't you think you should stay low?" Apple squeaks. "We don't have a giant bat to catch us when she disappears this time."

"I didn't imagine this Nevermore!" Raven shouts over the rushing wind. "She's the real thing! Good girl, Nevermore! Good, good girl!"

Dragon and girls soar into the air over Ever After High, circle the school once, and come to a landing in the courtyard outside the main gates. The ground shudders and the fierce wind subsides. The surrounding fog vanishes in an instant, and the horizon rolls with the green hills of Ever After.

"You have a lot of hexplaining to do, Ms. Queen!" Headmaster Grimm shouts as Raven and her friends leap off Nevermore's back.

The headmaster is marching toward them as if he intends to punish the cobblestones under his feet for poor roadway performance.

"I'm sorry?" Raven asks.

"An apology is not going to cut it this time, young lady," he says.

"I think perhaps Raven didn't understand what

she was being asked to hexplain," Apple says, pushing a lock of hair from her forehead and tucking it behind an ear. Despite a headlong run from a volcano and a frantic dragon ride, that single lock of hair was the only thing out of place. Her bare feet don't even look dirty.

Headmaster Grimm throws up his hands. "Hexplain? How about we begin with your abduction of the school council copresidents?"

Raven clenches her fists. Her magic is back, crackling around her fingertips. After all she's been through, she has a good mind to turn him into a frog.

"Oh, we weren't abducted," Apple says.

"*I was!*" Maddie shouts, grinning.

"But," Apple says, raising a hand to stall whatever words are about to come out of Headmaster Grimm's mouth, "not by Raven."

"*Oooh, nonono*, not by our sweet little Ravenbird!" Maddie says. Her voice lowers to a conspiratorial whisper. "I was kidnapped by the shambling zombibos!"

"Zomboyz," Raven corrects.

"Zomboyz!" Maddie repeats. "Because of my special listening powers, I was questioned with spray bottles and made to divulge the location of the secret base!"

"That's...not quite right," Raven says.

"Of course it isn't. *Nothing* is quite right, or everything would be quite boring." Maddie nods smartly. "But there *was* a spray bottle."

Headmaster Grimm holds up a finger. "No more Hattersplaining, if you please. I would like the straight story without the nonsense."

Raven shrugged. "There was trouble," she says.

"And it was taken care of," Apple says.

"*Spelltacularly*," Maddie adds.

"And the...er...others?" Headmaster Grimm asks. "The *monster* girls?"

"They're gone," Raven says, and her voice catches at the end, because someone else is gone, too.

Apple takes a deep breath. "They are back home. We hope. Everything is fine, Headmaster Grimm, really. Everyone is fine. All is back to normal."

Headmaster Grimm clears his throat with a *harrumph*. "It had better be. Normal and fine are the glue that holds us together."

"*Headmaster Grimm!*"

A little man who works as a groundskeeper for Ever After High calls from a clutch of bushes near the fountain. "The azaleas have begun to sing again! The new fertilizer didn't work!"

"Which song are they singing?" Headmaster Grimm asks.

"'Rubber Baby Buggy Bumpers,' I think," the little man says. "I don't know azalea tunes well."

"That's just typical," Headmaster Grimm mutters. "On top of everything, now this."

"All is normal," Apple says, gently turning Headmaster Grimm toward the groundskeeper and his bushes. "All is fine."

"*Fine*," says Raven. She sighs. "I can't believe she's gone."

"Oh, Drac's back at Monster High, I bet!" Maddie says. "Let me check. Hey, Brooke! Are Drac and Frankie back at Monster High safe and sound?"

The Narrator does not speak to Maddie, not in any real way. That part of the story, of how Draculaura and Frankie return home, has yet to be told. Moreover, the Narrator knows that *any* connection between the two lands, any at all, could be dangerous.

Anything that might narrow the Margins between worlds could risk a lava rise and undo everything the characters worked for.

"Yeah, so Brooke says we can't talk about it," Maddie says. "It's dangerous to bring worlds together…blah blah lava and so on. But she *did* say the story of how Draculaura and Frankie return home hasn't been told *yet*, which means they *do* get home. So there you go."

Madeline Hatter is awfully clever.

Raven smiles at her friend, but she wasn't talking about Draculaura, and Apple knows it. She takes Raven's arm, and they walk side by side up to their room.

"She saved us," Apple says. "She saved everything. I wasn't sure she would."

"Me neither," Raven says. "I think she likes… or…liked that. Oh curses. I don't like how this feels."

"I know. I'm sorry. It's a terrible way to feel."

"*Pluuus,*" Maddie says, slipping between them to take both their arms, "no one is ever really gone."

"Not when we remember them," Apple says.

"Not when their stories are told," says Raven.

"You know what? I wasn't sure what I would do in the future after I graduate—"

"You mean if you decide not to do what I've been telling you to do all these years?" Apple asks.

"Poisoning you with an apple is still off the table," Raven says. "No, I think I'll write. Tell stories."

They enter their dorm room, and Apple goes straight to her floor-length mirror. "Hey, Raven? Worth a shot?"

Raven takes a deep breath and then performs the spell that connects this mirror to the mirror prison.

The Evil Queen, spiky shoulder pads, headdress and all, is sitting inside it, looking royally cheesed off.

"Yay, Readers," says the Evil Queen, her chin in her hands. "Thanks *a lot*."

Raven laughs.

Kitty comes into their room, her purple hair wild and unbrushed, her eyes bleary. "I think I overslept. My alarm didn't go off this morning. Has anyone seen my clock?"

CHAPTER 30

I<small>T'S MORNING AT</small> M<small>ONSTER</small> H<small>IGH</small>. T<small>HE ANCIENT</small> building sits up on Monster Hill, mysterious and yet inviting, like a story just waiting to happen.[79] The cemetery stones gleam, the roof is as shiny as a coin, the bats in the attic are humming in their sleep. Everything seems new, fresh, fixed up, and happy—in a gloriously boo-tiful way.

And around the school grounds there's a definite lack of mist. From the front steps, the view extends for miles and miles across a land that just wants to forget about that weird wall of fog that ominously

---

79 *Ooh*, that was a bookmarkable sentence, much better than the opening sentences I wrote in chapter 1. I really am improving!

descended over everything and then just as quickly disappeared again yesterday as soon as Frankie and Draculaura came home from wherever they'd been.[80]

The two ghouls aren't divulging those secrets as they hurry to history class.

"Hey, Drac?" Frankie clears her throat. "You know, I'll understand if you don't want to be my best ghoulfriend anymore. You got along so great with Raven. There are dozens of monsters at Monster High now. You don't have to stick with me just 'cause I was the only one at first. And I know I messed up our presentation. I'm new at ... at *everything*, trying to figure stuff out, and I just can't be perfect—"

"Perfect?" says Draculaura. "Who needs perfect? You're a scientist. Scientists make mistakes all the time! Thousands of mistakes before they make great discoveries. I read that somewhere."

"Yeah, but—"

"Frankie Stein, you are a silly monster. Now, let's do an absolutely horrific presentation together, shall we?"

Frankie smiles, but the smile drops away when

---

80 I still write pretty long sentences sometimes. Oh well.

they stand up in the front of the room. Once again the entire class is staring at her—some with black eyes, some blue, some red, some with eyeballs waving on the tips of tentacles. Their teacher, Mr. Rotter, folds his arms.

Frankie smiles sheepishly.

From the back row, Clawdeen Wolf gives her two claws up. Frankie smiles wider. She glances at Draculaura, who nods encouragingly. They haven't had time to prepare a new, exciting, creeptastic presentation—you know, since they spent most of the past couple of days journeying through eerie land-scapes, battling deadly villains, barely escaping with their lives, and all that.

A tiny thorn of regret twinges in Frankie's chest. A report on Shadow High would be *just* the kind of earth-cracking, jaw-dropping, thrilling presenta-tion she had hoped for all along. But Frankie and Draculaura agreed that it's also the one thing they can't talk about. The more people who know about Shadow High and the other lands of the World of Stories, the more likely someone will try to cross lands. Any crossing back and forth risks pulling the lands closer together. With the lands separated, the Unmaking stays down deep in the trenches.

Maybe someday someone will figure out a way to safely unite all the lands. Until then...

"Our report is on... Normie High!" says Frankie.

The class applauds politely.

Frankie and Drac take turns delivering fascinating facts about Normie High.

"In Normie High, the kids use things called 'drinking fountains' to drink... *water*!"

"*Ohhhh*," says the class.

"In Normie High, their lockers are shaped like tall, skinny rectangles!"

"*Aaaah*," says the class.

When they wrap up their presentation, Draculaura looks at Frankie with a raised eyebrow. Frankie nods. They agreed to a single special effect.

"The End!" says Draculaura. She presses a button on the EffecTacular.

A small burst of fireworks brightens the gloomy classroom with purple, red, and blue sparks of light.

"*Oooooh*," says the class.

Frankie smiles. Purple for Raven, red for Apple, and blue for Maddie. Draculaura smiles, too, reaching out to take Frankie's hand, the new hand her dad attached last night. They stare at the pretty light show, smiling contentedly, until they notice that some of the fireworks sparks landed on Mr. Rotter's desk and his papers are crackling with flames. Frankie is prepared this time and presses the SIMULATED SWAMP WATER button. The fire fizzles out with a puff of gray smoke.

Their classmates jump to their feet, claws, and hooves, applauding wildly. Mr. Rotter rolls his eyes. Draculaura laughs.

"We did it!" says Draculaura.

"It wasn't perfect," Frankie says.

"Eh, perfect is boring."

EPILOGUE

THE NOISES OUTSIDE FRANKIE'S BEDROOM window usually help her sleep. Frogs croaking, witches cackling, wolves howling, and the wet, slurping footfalls of Unseen Things all combine to make a soothing backdrop to her rest. But not tonight. Tonight the frogs are too loud, the witches too annoying, and the wolves too shrill. The slow tread of Unseen Things is nice, but it isn't enough to drown out everything else.

The electric spinning compass is on her nightstand, a memento from an adventure that is already fading from memory. The compass is useless now, of course. Raven's enchantment has worn off. And the chisel that was in it is now far away, safe in its socket at Shadow High.

Frankie opens Apple's backpack. Besides the Mapalogue and the Skullette, there are a few other Apple-y items: a new notebook full of crisp white paper, a sweater in case of a chill, a hat in case of sun, her outdoors-wear tiara, and a packet of unsalted nuts. On a lark, Frankie sticks the tiara in the compass and flips on the power switch. It whirs, the electric motor working just as it should. No magic now, but the soft hum of the machine is soothing, and it drowns out the louder croaks and cackles, so she leaves it on.

And after Frankie drifts to sleep, sometime between night's depths and its shallows, a spark grows around the tiara. A soft green pulses from the compass, and if someone were watching, they'd see the glow form the barest hint of an arrow pointing west.

ABOUT THE AUTHORS

Shannon Hale and Dean Hale are the *New York Times* bestselling wife-and-husband writing team behind The Princess in Black series, *The Unbeatable Squirrel Girl: Squirrel Meets World,* and the graphic novel *Rapunzel's Revenge.* Shannon is also the author of books like *The Goose Girl,* Newberry Honor–winner *Princess Academy, Real Friends,* and *Ever After High: The Storybook of Legends.*[1] Dean and Shannon are thrilled to be writing this book together, especially since "a clash of monsters and fairytales" is also an apt description for their marriage. They live in Utah, where they herd their four young children, write books, and perform in a punk rock band named Rat Muzzle.[2]

---

1 Also some other Ever After High books that my parents narrated: *The Unfairest of Them All, A Wonderlandiful World,* and *Once Upon a Time.* They are *so good,* but don't tell my parents I said so, or they might get big-headed about it.

2 Um...I think they're kidding about the punk rock band thing. *Ooh,* if I had a punk band, I'd call it Figure of Screech. Or maybe Scream of Consciousness. No lie, my dad is part of a barbershop quartet named the Narratones. What would you call your band?

MONSTER

Ever After High

Wonderland

EXSTO MONSTRUM
EXSTO MONSTRUM

N

W   E

S